ZOMBIE TRAIN

ZOMBIE TRAIN

David Macinnis Gill

 Greenwillow Books
An Imprint of HarperCollins*Publishers*

Zombie Train
Copyright © 2024 by David Macinnis Gill

The text of this book is set in 12-point Adobe Caslon Pro.
Book design by Paul Zakris

Library of Congress Cataloging-in-Publication Data

Names: Gill, David Macinnis, author.
Title: Zombie train / by David Macinnis Gill.
Description: First edition. |
New York : Greenwillow Books, an Imprint of HarperCollins Publishers, 2024. |
Audience: Ages 8-12. |
Summary: While twelve-year-old Wyatt rides out the zombie apocalypse on his crew's cobbled together train, a mysterious girl arrives with stories of a potential cure for the zombie parasite.
Identifiers: LCCN 2023053841 (print) | LCCN 2023053842 (ebook) |
ISBN 9780063116511 (hardcover) | ISBN 9780063116535 (ebook)
Subjects: CYAC: Zombies—Fiction. | Survival—Fiction. |
Railroad Travel—Fiction. | LCGFT: Zombie fiction. | Novels.
Classification: LCC PZ7.G39854 Zo 2024 (print) | LCC PZ7.G39854 (ebook) |
DDC [Fic]—dc23
LC record available at https://lccn.loc.gov/2023053841
LC ebook record available at https://lccn.loc.gov/2023053842
24 25 26 27 28 LBC 5 4 3 2 1
First Edition

GREENWILLOW BOOKS

FOR AMY F. KING

1

WYATT

Everything you think you know about zombies is wrong. Zombies are alive and unwell and want to eat your face. But not your brains. They don't have the dexterity or tools to open your cranium. Oh, and the zombie virus? No such thing. It's not a virus but a parasite, a tiny protozoan that spreads via your brain's pathways. It actually *does* eat your brain.

Now, a zombie will absolutely chow down your arm or leg. At least at first, when they're bloodlusty and move so fast your eyes can't track them.

The first zombie phase is called zombie fresh. There's no outrunning a zombie fresh. Just hope they're chasing somebody slower than you.

The second zombie phase is the longest. They're what we call shamblers because they have a shambling gait. They're hungry like fresh, but rot has set in. Their coordination's way off—their lizard brain's gone haywire—so we outrun them easy, but they can stampede faster than a cattle herd.

The last zombie phase is the ugliest. The shambler's connective tissue dissolves, and it melts into a glob of greasy zombie guts. A Humpty Dumpty.

Wyatt had never seen a Humpty Dumpty up close and personal.

Until today.

From the engine of the zombie train, Denver's Union Pacific North Yard looked like a mess of spaghetti strands, penned in by collapsing service buildings and rusting freight cars covered with grime. More like a graveyard than a railyard. The weather was sunny and 83°, unseasonably warm for October. Ahead, the tracks disappeared under a mishmash of freeway bridges, and in the distance Wyatt spotted a weird shape sitting right on the track switch.

"Shut. The. Front. Door." Wyatt zoomed in with binoculars. "Conductor, we need a cleanup on aisle five," he said, thumbing the mic.

Wyatt stood in the freight train's cab next to the engineer, Pez. His leg bounced as he stared at the shape in the distance. This was his first switch throw as a brakeman. He didn't want to screw it up.

"Wyatt?" Marti's voice crackled over the speakers. She got her daily iron supplement eating nails for breakfast. "Cleanup on aisle five? Is that a joke?"

"No. I mean, yes, but I'm not joking." His chest tightened with worry. Why had he tried to be funny? "It's what Pike used to say."

"Your brother's conductor days are done, so get over it," Marti said. "What's the situation? We good to go or not?"

"Negative, boss," he said, feeling like a scolded toddler. "A zombie's sitting on the switch. It's a Humpty Dumpty."

"I'm busy in the caboose," she said. "Get Cheddar to lend a hand."

She was in the caboose? That couldn't mean anything good. Was she trying to sabotage him? Clearing the track was hard work, and Cheddar wasn't into physical labor. "Maybe Tuna instead?" Wyatt said. "He's fourth up."

"Tuna's busy, and Cheddar's third up, right after you." Her voice turned icy. "Unless you want Diesel."

I'd rather smooch a zombie fresh, Wyatt thought. "I'll take Cheddar," he said, his voice rising. He exhaled to let the nerves pass and switched to public address mode. "Cheddar, cleanup on aisle five. Bring Twinkies."

He hung the mic up and focused the field glasses on the zombie plopped on the track a mile or so ahead. "Pez, you won't believe this."

"More bighorn sheep?" Pez asked from the control box. He was a beanpole with stilts for legs. Chopped-up curly black hair full of cowlicks. Brown face covered with grease. He wore a white tank top and overalls, which stank of sweat and diesel fuel. "Or a buffalo herd?"

"Look for yourself."

Pez leaned out the side window. "Too fat to be no deer," he said. "Not shaggy enough for buffalo."

"It's a Humpty Dumpty!" Wyatt felt his anxiety turn to exasperation. "Wearing a Dolly Parton wig."

"How'd an ol' Dumpty make it 'cross the rail yard?" Pez

sounded the air horn three times—a warning. "What's with the wig?"

"I'm psychic now? Slow Lucille down." Wyatt thumbed the PA again, anxious to get the job done. "Cheddar! Stop stalling!"

Pez eased the brake valve. Air hissed out the pipes. Lucille was the train's name, and her locomotive was a yellow-and-black diesel, model DDA40X. Her riders had one unbreakable rule, and Marti enforced it ruthlessly. *Never stop the zombie train.*

"Three-quarters mile to the switch," Pez said.

"Give me a head start." Wyatt gave Pez a fist bump and opened the side door. He felt a rush of cold air. He wanted to prove that he wasn't just Pike's little brother. That he could stand on his own two size-thirteen feet. "With Cheddar helping, we need all the time we can get."

Pez puckered up. "Thought you and Cheddar was best friends."

"One and only best friends, and Ched's the smartest kid on the train. Maybe the world." Wyatt grabbed a coal shovel and got ready to jump from the footboard. "But it doesn't make him run fast."

True, Cheddar was the slowest runner on the train, but he'd also saved Wyatt's bacon so many times, they'd never be square. "I take it back, Pez," he said, tugging on the yellow band around his wrist. "What I said."

The engineer nodded. "It's took back."

If everything went according to plan, the train would follow a spur from Denver to Cheyenne and then continue on the northern loop. Lucille would travel from Colorado to Wyoming to Utah and back. One big circle. It was how they survived, three hundred and fifty-seven days after the outbreak, and surviving was all that mattered.

"Wyatt!" Cheddar's footsteps clomped on the engine decking. He was pear-shaped, with wispy blond hair and a face so pink cheeked, he looked like a middle-school Gerber baby. He wore khaki pants and a blue polo that he tugged down like a window shade. "Don't leave!"

"Hurry!" Wyatt yelled. Last time they'd rolled through the North Yard, he'd helped Pike with the switch, and it had gone flawlessly. Now he'd settle for just keeping the train on the tracks. "Before Marti chews our butts to nubs."

"Sorry, Wy. Had to finish the soup." Cheddar was panting when he reached the ladder. "The littles get cranky when lunch is late."

"Next time let Tater handle the soup?" Wyatt had never wanted to be second-in-command of a train loaded with orphans. He never wanted a zombie apocalypse either, only a normal life with his mom and his brother. But you play the hand you're dealt. "We've got to throw that switch now or—"

"Wyatt!" Pez yelled. "Engine two's losing compression,

ASAP! I gotta fix it ASAP, and we're clean outta bubble gum and baling wire!"

"That's two ASAPs, and you only get one," Wyatt said, more impatient than ever. Pez was always crying wolf about Lucille's health. If it wasn't a flummox in the engine, it was a gremlin in the hydraulics.

"Lucille's been limping since the Flatirons." Pez pointed at a gauge blinking red. "If the Big Ten switchback turns hadn't been downhill, engine two woulda blowed."

"I'll tell Marti after we throw the switch," Wyatt said. "Ched! Count of three, we jump. Three!"

The air horn sounded. Wyatt jumped off the side ladder and hit the ground running. Cheddar climbed down gingerly. His foot slipped on the bottom rung, and he fell onto the embankment, teetering toward Lucille's churning wheels.

"Cheddar!" Wyatt yelled. "Watch out!"

"Huh?"

"Move!"

Wyatt tackled Cheddar, and they rolled down the rocky embankment, an instant before Lucille's wheels could amputate Cheddar's toes. Their most valuable rider had almost died, and it was Wyatt's fault. What would Pike have said if he'd seen that epic screwup?

"Can you believe my luck?" Cheddar said before his knees buckled, too.

Of course Wyatt could believe it. He'd just seen it. "First rule of clearing track, Ched? Always keep your feet," he said as he scrambled up and raced ahead, zigzagging between endless lines of rusting boxcars. "Hurry! We've got seven minutes before Lucille reaches the switch!"

Cheddar checked his watch. "Seven minutes, thirty-eight seconds to be precise."

"Brake Dude!" a voice called. Behind them, a scrawny, greasy-haired kid jumped down from the engine's back ladder. "Diesel said for me to tag along."

"Not Festus," Cheddar said, gasping for breath. He was definitely better at making soup than running. "Festus is a walking demolition crew, and since when does Diesel give orders?"

"Since never." Wyatt clenched his jaw. Everything about Diesel got on his nerves. His rotten attitude. His giving orders when he was only fifth up. "It's a free country!" he yelled back at Festus. "If you want to be a zombie's lunch buddy, you're welcome to get eaten!"

Festus landed in a gully, then popped to his feet, knocking prairie grass from his shirt. "Meant to do that." He wore a stained tie-dye T-shirt and baggy jeans. His stringy red hair was tucked beneath an oily ball cap. The bill hid a pasty face so sharp-nosed and pointy, he looked like an underfed sewer rat.

"Follow orders, Festus," Wyatt yelled, feeling the weight

of the train—and expectations—bearing down on him. "Or you get two days of latrine duty."

Festus bowed his head. A hint of shame crossed his face, only to be replaced by a smile. "Might be worth cleaning toilets to grind your nerves."

"Suit yourself," Wyatt said and swung the coal shovel over his shoulder. "Come on, Ched! Let's go! Pick up the pace!"

Two hundred yards later, Wyatt reached the zombie. The Humpty Dumpty weighed three hundred pounds, easy. Dressed in overalls with no shirt. Its fleshy pumpkin head was covered with a wig of yellow hair.

Still panting, Cheddar looked back at the looming locomotive. "Lucille's closing fast."

Wyatt poked the fridge-sized gelatinous lump with the shovel. The blade sank into the Dumpty's belly. This one was more ripe than usual, and he'd never seen one dressed in a wig and wearing lipstick.

"What a sick joke," Wyatt said, "playing dress-up with a dying thing."

But was it a joke? They hadn't run into humans in Denver the last two loop runs. Before that, they'd seen stragglers. On overpasses. Near campfires. In fenced parking lots. Were there any kids left?

A screeching howl interrupted Wyatt's thoughts. On the overpass that spanned the yard, dozens of shambling zombies pressed against the chain-link fence. Thick as flies, they screamed as they tried to break through the wire.

"Were those there a minute ago?" he asked Cheddar.

"Not that many." Cheddar pointed at the road leading to the overpass. "More are on the way."

"A shambler convention. Just what we need." Wyatt tried to play it off, but so many zombies made him jumpy. He handed the shovel to Cheddar, then pulled on the switch handle until his face turned red. "Won't budge."

"Brute force won't work, Wy," Cheddar said. "Use the shovel to lever the Dumpty off."

Festus grabbed for the shovel. "I'll help."

"No, we've got this," Wyatt said, cramming the shovel under the Humpty's flabby backside.

The metal tip stuck, like it was buried in concrete, and the zombie snorked.

Wyatt twisted the wooden handle. "Ched, gimme a hand."

Cheddar grasped the shovel. Together, they leaned hard on the grip. After a few seconds, the zombie rocked forward, and its buttocks lifted off the ground.

"Steady pressure," Wyatt said. "Don't want to break—"

"Dog pile!" Festus screamed and dived on them.

Crack!

The handle snapped in half. All three boys hit the ground hard, and Lucille rolled on unmercifully, her shadow looming as she blocked out the sun.

2

RYLE

When zombie screams reached her hiding spot, Ryle hopped up to have a look. She knocked damp straw off her pants and eased open the boxcar door. Whoa. Zombies were swarming the Pecos Street overpass. Just like Parcheesi had planned.

At three p.m., a horn sounded three times.

Finally, she thought, the zombie train has arrived.

"Is it them?" Vash whispered, and sat up, on high alert. A minute ago she'd been dead asleep. The girl had ears like a rabbit and eyes like a hawk. "Is it the right train?"

What other train could it be? Ryle bit her tongue. No reason to set off Vash's temper. "Shh. Don't wake the littles yet. In case there's a fight."

Ryle peered through the doors again. From here, she could see the glob zombie sitting on the rails where the switch should be. She didn't understand how it got there, but it didn't take a genius to know it was Parcheesi's doing.

Vash joined her at the door. "What's it look like?"

"Stay inside." Ryle nudged her back into the shadows. "If they spot us, Parcheesi's plans will be blown."

"Girl, they ain't seen me," Vash said.

"Parcheesi said the guy in charge is superhuman."

"Huh. Sounds like one of her stories to me." Vash shook her head. "You know she exaggerates to make stuff sound scary."

"Never say that to her." Ryle knew that Vash wasn't Parcheesi's biggest fan. "Gear up and be ready for my signal."

"You're the boss." Vash bumped Ryle's fist, and they waggled their fingers like their fists had exploded. "Till Parcheesi gets back."

Ryle tensed up, irritated. Even though Vash was teasing, it was true. Until Parcheesi joined them a couple of months ago, Ryle had been boss. Now she was Parcheesi's second, and that rubbed her wrong.

While Vash got ready, Ryle checked her own gear.

Rope? Check.

Knife? Check.

Attitude? Ch—

Voices.

Her ears perked up.

She heard two, no, three voices. One low and the others higher pitched. Then she heard footsteps. The first kid came into view—a tall boy with olive skin and dark hair. He wore a cowboy hat, a gun belt, and fancy boots. Seriously? He reached the glob zombie first and tried to throw the switch. Nothing happened. The tracks didn't budge. Two more boys ran into view. A big kid, wheezing. A little one, hopping around like a caffeinated bullfrog.

These were the superhumans Parcheesi was all worried about? Ryle watched, laughing to herself, as the boys dog-piled a shovel and landed in a tangle of arms and legs.

"They're clueless," Ryle whispered to Vash. "I got this."

"And I got you, but . . . " Vash paused. "You ain't having second thoughts about—well, you know?"

Truth? Ryle had had second thoughts every time Parcheesi talked about Nirvana, but she'd survived the wasteland for months, fighting feral kids for food, water, and safe places to sleep. It had worn her down, and she needed a reason to hope.

"Too late for second thoughts," she said, as much to herself as Vash. "You want to live, don't you?"

Vash shrugged. "We all going to die at some point."

"Not before," Ryle said and slid the boxcar door open, "we get a chance to live."

3

WYATT

Festus pointed to the broken shovel protruding from the Dumpty's buttocks. "Talk about an atomic wedgie."

"Not funny," Cheddar said. He was not one to laugh in the face of danger.

Lucille's horn sounded again, filling the train yard. It was answered by a sudden, earsplitting shriek. Wyatt's blood ran cold, and all three boys looked to an overpass above the yard, where the chain-link fence had begun bending from the zombies massing against it. If it fell, the herd would devour the train and everybody on it.

Wyatt stared for several seconds, then another blood-curdling scream jolted him into action. "Quick! You're the physics genius!" he said to Cheddar. "How do we eject that zombie?"

"A lever."

"Ched! We just tried that." And failed. Wyatt felt his confidence melt. Focus on the job, he thought. Ignore the zombies! Focus on the train!

The Dumpty listed to the side like a cow chewing its cud. Except it wasn't a cud. The zombie was eating its own tongue.

Wyatt closed his eyes, but he couldn't block out the wet, squishy chewing that made him want to hurl. "Let's push it!" he said.

Cheddar shrugged. "If we push on the Dumpty, its skin will rupture."

"It'll pop like a stinky grape?" Festus' eyes lit up. "Woohoo! Let's poke the zombie! Diesel said Dumpties is full of soup."

"More like putrefied Jell-O." Cheddar put his glasses back on. "Or haggis."

Festus poked the Dumpty, then smelled his finger. "What's hair gas?" His lips puckered up like he'd sucked a rotten lemon.

"Haggis." Cheddar adjusted his glasses. "A Scottish pudding of oatmeal, suet, and cow organs boiled in a sheep's stomach."

"You two knock it off!" Wyatt said. "Do you not see the train barreling down on us? The bloodthirsty zombies up there on the overpass?"

"Sweet!" Festus scurried away. "I'll find a stick to poke it."

"Sorry, Wy," Cheddar said.

Wyatt held out his hand. "Twinkie."

"Twinkie?"

"To bait the zombie!"

"Twinkie." Cheddar pulled a snack cake from his pocket. "Two minutes, one second until impact from the train."

"Don't say 'impact.'" Wyatt waved the spongy cake under the Dumpty's nostrils till it snorked to life. "You know you waaaant it."

The zombie came at Wyatt with its nose. Not its arms. Not its legs. Not even with its brown, craggy teeth. Just a nose that it tried to use as a spear. Poor thing. It wasn't its fault it had turned. It was still a living human being. It wasn't dead.

Yet.

Wyatt pulled the cake away, but the Dumpty still didn't budge. "Ched, stand clear. In case it gets hinky," he said. He heard Marti's voice in his head. *Do your job. Just do your job.*

Cheddar backed up. "Clear."

"Found one!" Festus ran toward them with a branch. "Can I poke the hair gas?"

"No, you'll put your eye out," Wyatt said. "And poking's disrespectful to the person the Dumpty used to be."

Festus pursed his lips, the tumbleweeds in his brain tumbling. "Was it respectful to whack it with the shovel?" He jabbed Cheddar's belly. "Cheeseboy's stuffed with hair gas, too."

"Wyatt! Cheddar!" Marti's voice echoed from Lucille's external speakers. "Stop screwing around! Throw that switch!"

Behind them the air horn sounded, and air brakes hissed. Lucille's horn blasted three more times, which was Pez code for *You're going to die.*

Festus laughed maniacally. "So the train misses the

15

switch," he said. "Big freaking deal. Ain't life or death."

"Stop!" Wyatt snatched Festus' stick. "Let's gang tackle it. It's our only chance."

Lucille's horn blasted again, and the zombies on the overpass screeched in response, and Wyatt's hair stood on end. Then on the overpass, Wyatt spotted something terrifying. Bodies streaking along at inhuman speeds, scaling the fence.

"Zombie fresh!" Festus yelled.

The most dangerous and vicious of all zombies—lightning fast, murderous, and hungry. They reached the razor wire, shoving their arms and chests against it, ignoring the chunks of flesh being torn off. Under their weight, the fencing buckled. How could there be so many zombie fresh here? Why had they swarmed to this spot?

"One minute!" Cheddar said, eyes locked on his watch.

"Train's coming! Woo-hoo!" Festus grabbed the stick back. "Better poke it fast!"

"Shut it!" Wyatt yelled over the zombie shrieks, his mind pinballing.

"Ahem," a voice came from behind them. "You boys sure like to cut it close."

Wyatt's head snapped around.

A stranded stood behind them.

A girl.

Pointing a wooden bō right at his face.

4

WYATT

The girl holding the staff had spiked purple hair and brown skin and wore faded jeans, a red Henley under a wool sweater, and Iron Ranger boots. She looked like a catalog model—until she pressed the bō against his left nostril. "One twitch, and I'll bust your nose like a ripe cantaloupe."

"Hi?" Wyatt said, surprised how calm he sounded.

The girl waved Wyatt aside. "Move."

"Don't take another step!" Festus whimpered, waving the stick. "I ain't afraid to use this!"

"You're afraid of your own shadow." The girl slipped a lasso off her shoulder. "There's lots of dead out here, kid." She pointed to the zombie fresh pushing through the razor wire. "Care to be one of them?"

The train horn sounded. Lucille was right there. Right! There! Barreling down on them! The girl was marching straight to the Dumpty. "Thanks for the offer," Wyatt yelled and ran after her, "but we've got this."

"Must be why your train's about to wreck." She looked back, face part smirk and part sneer. "My name's Ryle. You're Wyatt, Cheddar, and Fester, and you're all boneheads." Ryle lassoed the Dumpty, then whistled through her fingers. "Vash! Tie this off!"

Another girl jumped from a boxcar and caught the

tossed rope. She was smaller than Ryle, with a darker complexion and high cheekbones. Her hair was dyed, too, and shaved on the sides. She wore a brown Henley, heavy boots, and hiking khakis.

Cheddar checked the switch, then his watch. "Thirty seconds!"

Vash tied the rope around her waist, then climbed back up the boxcar. She flashed the thumbs-up.

"Vash, when I say jump," Ryle commanded. "*Jump*."

"The Dumpty's innards are mush," Wyatt said. "The rope will just slice it in half."

"Innards? What TV western did you escape from?" Ryle turned and barked, "Vash! Jump!"

"Ten seconds." Cheddar's voice cracked. "Nine."

Vash jumped, and the rope went tight. The lasso cut through flesh, and the Dumpty snorted in surprise. Wyatt was about to say *I told you so* when the zombie made a squishy gurgle noise like Spam ejected from the can.

It tumbled off the tracks.

"Now!" Ryle yelled.

Wyatt yanked the pull rod, and the track switched just as Lucille rolled past the switch. Not a second to spare.

"We did it!" Cheddar dropped to the ground. "Too close. Too close."

Ryle squatted beside the Dumpty and cut the rope with a multi-tool. Then she did the necessary thing to end its misery.

"Quick thinking," Wyatt said, not even trying to hide his admiration.

"Rope cuts skin, not bone." She offered him a handshake. "Even the squishy ones still have spines. Unlike some humans."

"Ouch." Wyatt flinched. "Do you usually jump right into zombie removal?"

"Zombie removal. Zombie herd feeding frenzy." She slid the bō under a strap on her back while Vash coiled the rope. "One call does it all."

She reminded him a little of Marti—skilled but arrogant. He owed her a solid, no doubt about it, and honor demanded payback. A hot meal was the least he could offer, right?

"I'm Wyatt."

"I'm still Ryle."

Lucille's horn sounded three times in quick succession as Pez flashed a thumbs-up. Wyatt watched Lucille veer to the right, blowing dust as she passed. He counted twelve cars after the locomotive—fuel car, map car, sightseer lounge, dining car, infirmary, three sleepers, two boxcars, and an open flatcar for vehicles, trailed by the bright red caboose.

Marti stood atop the caboose. She was short for almost thirteen, with light brown skin and curly hair, and she was dressed in body armor. Jaw set. Arms crossed. Staring hard.

Wyatt's heart sank. That meant he'd pay for his screwup. "That's our cue," he said, feeling strangely optimistic. He'd failed, but it wasn't the end of the world. The zombie train was still running the loop. "Thanks for the help, still Ryle."

"You're welcome," she said. "Wyatt. Cheddar. Fester."

"It's Festus!" Festus whined.

"I call 'em like I see 'em," Ryle said. "So long, boys. Don't get yourselves eaten."

Wyatt wasn't ready to let Ryle go. They could use a fighter like her. "We owe you for saving us, and there's plenty of food on Lucille."

Cheddar cut him a look—only the conductor could invite strandeds to ride. He pulled Wyatt aside. "Maybe you're being hasty."

"It's just one meal."

"Isn't it convenient that these two showed up in the nick of time? Who put the Dumpty on the tracks? What about the deer carcasses?"

Wyatt whispered, "What deer carcasses?"

"The ones near the railyard overpasses, Captain Oblivious. You saw Marti on the caboose? She's . . . displeased."

Wyatt tugged at his yellow wristband, a nervous tick he'd inherited from his mom. "Marti doesn't scare me." Which was a bald-faced lie.

"She scares you, me, and the rest of the riders. The only

one who didn't fear her was Pike, and you know what happened to him." Cheddar caught himself. "I'm sorry. That was insensitive."

"Yo, Wyatt," Vash called. "We might be interested in some grub. But it depends."

"On?" Wyatt asked.

Vash knocked dust off her clothes. "On what kind of train you got. Know what I'm saying?"

Wyatt had no idea what Vash was saying. "It's a . . . train?"

"It's a train! Hear that, Ryle? Your boy says it's a train." Vash laughed and leaned on Ryle's shoulder. "Ryle's top dog of our crew. Why'd she want to ride with y'all boneheads?"

Vash's laugh echoed across the rail yard, and the zombies on the overpass responded by screeching louder than ever. Wyatt's blood ran cold.

"I rescind the invitation," Wyatt said, tipping his hat to Ryle, his tone more stern than he intended. He wanted to sound calm, but inside, the urge to run made him itch. "Lucille doesn't stop for anybody."

Ryle stared at him, and Wyatt felt himself relax. Her eyes were big and brown and unblinking. Her mouth knitted into a frown, like she was thinking with her face. "Vash," she said. "Call the kids."

Vash whistled. "Step up and mount up!"

Four kids jumped from Vash's boxcar. They were littles,

all younger than eight, dressed like they'd stepped from a magazine. But their hungry faces were dirty, thin, and drawn. They definitely needed a hot meal. Baths, too. Marti was not going to be happy. A couple of skilled fighters was one thing, but six mouths to feed?

Too bad. No matter how vexed Marti got, Wyatt never turned littles away.

"My crew." Ryle eyed Wyatt like she was trying to read him. "Got food for us all?"

"Plenty," Wyatt said before he was interrupted by a loud crash.

On the overpass, the fence collapsed. A wave of zombie fresh jumped from the bridge. They slammed to the ground, shattering bones, then rose and began lurching toward Lucille.

"Get left, get eat!" Festus sprinted for the moving train. "That's what Diesel always says!"

Wyatt turned to Ryle. "Can the little ones run?"

"Like deer," she said, waving for Vash and the kids to follow.

They all jumped the tracks and tore through the rocky dirt, sprinting after Ryle. Cheddar trudged behind, and Wyatt glanced back at him, then at the roof of the caboose.

Empty.

Marti had left her post.

Ryle reached the caboose as a pint-sized girl reached for the platform railing.

"Not the caboose!" Wyatt yelled. "It's . . . we . . . " He swept the little up and sprinted past the flatcar and ahead of Ryle to the second boxcar. He swung the girl inside. "Up you go!"

"Behind you," Ryle said and handed him a small boy.

Wyatt swung him onto the deck. A third kid went in, followed by Vash, who helped the fourth little aboard. He turned back to Cheddar, whose face was blister red, and pushed him onboard.

"Thanks, I . . . " Cheddar huffed, then pointed straight ahead—a concrete wall had magically risen from the ground. "Wy! Look out!"

A sign on the Washington Street bridge read:

ROAD ENDS

1000 FEET

You've got to be kidding me, Wyatt thought. "You first!" He offered Ryle a hand. "Get in!"

"Not a chance!" Ryle yelled.

"I'm trying to be polite!"

"In the zombie apocalypse," she screamed, "polite gets you killed!"

Can't argue that, Wyatt thought, and grabbed a ladder rung as a blur of color screamed past him and tackled Ryle, pulling her down toward the wheels of the moving train.

5

RYLE

Ryle and the zombie rolled down the gravel embankment, locked in combat. The zombie's mud-stained pedal pushers were ripped to shreds, just like its T-shirt emblazoned with the words FREE HUGS.

Ryle came up bleeding, a six-inch gash in her knee, making the zombie's eyes go wild. "No free hugs!" Ryle yelled. "I've got mouths to feed, and I don't mean yours."

The zombie's red eyes were so filled with blood, they bulged from the sockets. Just-turneds were the absolute worst. Stupid fast. Ferocious appetites. Rage machines.

"Zombie fresh!" Wyatt yelled from the boxcar. "They're vicious!"

"Way to state the obvious!" Ryle yelled, ramming an elbow into the zombie's gut.

Then she kicked it, popping out its knee. But the just-turned didn't flinch. This was no glob zombie.

"Any advice, armchair quarterback?" she called.

Was Wyatt actually going to watch from the sidelines after she'd saved the train's bacon—and Wyatt's, too? Wait. Deal with the problem at hand, the one trying to eat your face. Time to improvise. If she couldn't hurt the zombie, she'd take away the thing it required.

Air.

She went for its neck, but the zombie sank its teeth into her arm. The pain turned her stomach, mixed with terror, and instantly morphed into rage.

"Let go!" Ryle punched it twice, but its teeth were beartrap tight. "You walking piece of liver loaf!"

"Ched! Watch the kids!" Wyatt swung down from Lucille and sprinted toward Ryle. "Aim for the eyes!"

"It's the teeth that bite!"

"Never mind!" he yelled as he knocked the zombie off her.

The zombie growled and charged Wyatt, arms extended, moving at insane speed. Wyatt barely had time to duck and twirl as the zombie blew past him. It stopped short and snorted, confused by the sudden absence of prey.

Wyatt whistled.

The zombie wheeled, running low, loping like a mangy werewolf.

"Olé!" Wyatt said and slapped it with his hat as it rushed by.

Total bonehead move. Ryle reached for her bō but found only air. She turned in a quick circle, scanning the road—there! Ten feet away, half-buried in the grime. She grabbed it as the zombie charged again.

Wyatt sidestepped and swept its knee, the ligaments snapping like a chicken wing. For a second, Ryle felt a surge of excitement, but then the zombie swung an arm wildly, so fast, so vicious.

Its fist whacked Wyatt's jaw. He staggered backward. A wooden rail tie caught his heel, and he fell between the tracks. His skull clacked on the metal rail.

Come on, Wyatt, get up! she thought. But he was blinking like cartoon birds were circling his head. This was the guy who ran the train?

"Yo, tomato face!" Ryle screamed at the zombie. "Come get some!"

The zombie snorted at her but kept puppet-walking toward Wyatt, dragging its mangled leg behind.

She flung the bō.

Thwack.

The zombie stumbled as the staff cracked its skull. Red-black blood spurted out, and the rotter swayed back and forth, unable to stand, but unwilling to fall.

Wyatt got up slowly, favoring his twisted ankle and rubbing his head.

"Zombie's still alive," Ryle said.

"Let it live."

"It tried to eat me."

"Not its fault."

"We can't let it follow us." Ryle walked over and whacked the zombie's other knee. There was a crunch of bone, and it gurgled as it crumpled to the ground. "Happy?"

"That staff comes in handy," Wyatt said. "Crude but effective."

"Crude but effective is my motto." Ryle felt a stinging sensation and looked down at her torn sleeve. Blood was seeping out. She turned her forearm to get a better look. "Oops."

"Oops what?"

Ryle's heart hammered. The bite was bad. Saliva, that's how the virus spread. Don't whine, she told herself. Just get to Vash and tell her that it's up to her to find Nirv—

"That's no oops." Wyatt studied the wound. "We've got first aid on the train. Cheddar can fix it."

"Are you nuts?" Ryle drew back like he'd stung her. "Band-Aids won't stop me from turning into . . . " She couldn't say it.

"Into what?"

"Y'know, a zombie." Her mind was reeling. How could he act like it was nothing? He had to know what a bite meant. Even he couldn't be that naïve.

"Everything you know about zombies is wrong," Wyatt said, motioning for her to follow.

"Get bit, get turned," she said. How had she let this happen? She was so close to reaching their goal. "Everybody knows that."

"Haven't you been bitten before?"

"Like you have." The guy could hardly dress himself. How could he survive an attack?

Wyatt rolled up the sleeves of his denim shirt. His forearm was covered in so many bite wounds, his skin looked like a chewed-up corncob. "Albert Einstein was a really bad speller."

"That makes no sense."

"Neither does letting Lucille leave us," he said and jumped the embankment, hobbling on his sore ankle.

Ryle raced past him and reached the caboose first.

"Not the caboose!" he yelled. "Boxcar! Nobody goes to the caboose!"

That didn't sound ominous at all. She hated trusting him but had to board the train. Things had changed since Parcheesi rode the rails, like this new conductor Marti and someone named Wyatt that Parcheesi had never mentioned. Plus, the caboose windows were covered in foil. What were they hiding?

"Hey!" A blond boy with a bull neck waved Ryle toward the boxcar. "Over here!"

She grabbed his outstretched hand and swung herself inside. She landed on her feet, and the littles rushed in for a hug. Vash gave her a fist bump, then waggled her fingers like their fists had exploded.

"What took you so long?" Vash asked, then she nodded at the bull boy. "Atchway isthay erkjay."

"I'm Diesel," the boy said. "Resident jerk. What's your name, sweetheart?"

"Ryle, and I'm not your sweetheart."

Diesel shook her hand for too long. "Ryle. That's a weird name."

"Says the guy named for a petroleum by-product." Ryle easily broke his grip. "Where'd your mother give birth, a truck stop?"

Diesel winked and laughed, and she felt like a piece of zombie bait. The boy was built like a refrigerator. His skin was ashen white, and he had pale blue eyes and slicked down straw-colored hair. When he sweated, he stank of stale garlic, and he looked like he was always sweating.

She took a deep breath and inhaled a mouthful of Axe body spray. How could cologne that smelled like vinegar soaked in sweaty tennis shoes still be a thing? But even the cologne couldn't drown out his garlicky BO.

It was hate at first sight. She'd take Wyatt any day of the week. Wait! Wyatt! "Grab Wyatt!" she yelled.

"Almost forgot." Diesel leaned out and smirked at Wyatt—who was still running alongside Lucille—and spat a huge loogie. "Dodgeball!"

Wyatt ducked the wad of snot. "Jerk!" Then his toe caught a rock, and his ankle buckled.

Diesel knelt on the decking and stuck out a hand. "Last chance."

Wyatt took two strides and dived. Their fingertips touched. Then Diesel pulled his hand back.

"Sorry, dude," Diesel said. "Marti wants to teach you a lesson you'll never forget."

"What are you doing?" Ryle yelled. Anger rose in her throat, and she could barely contain a scream. What kind of kids would abandon their own? Parcheesi was right about them. They were animals, worse than ferals, and they deserved to lose the train.

She pushed Diesel aside, and her gaze met Wyatt's. He looked betrayed and confused, his wide eyes searching frantically for a lifeline that wasn't going to come.

6

WYATT

"Take my hand!" Ryle yelled, shoving Diesel aside.

You got one chance to jump, don't blow it, Wyatt thought, and felt a burst of adrenaline. His arm reaching full out, he wrapped his fingers around Ryle's wrist.

Her eyes widened with shock. "Look out!"

A thousand tons of concrete bridge was rushing right at his face. A whoosh of wind slapped him against the boxcar's corrugated sheathing again. Sound bounced between concrete and steel, Lucille's wheels screeching. His shirttail whacked the concrete wall as the train swept beneath the bridge, and the wind sucked his Stetson clean off.

So much for my favorite hat, Wyatt thought. He felt a pang of regret, but with a sigh of thanks, he swung inside the boxcar.

He collapsed into a pile of straw, body shaking. The boxcar smelled of coal tar and dust, and it was the best smell ever. As he lay on the decking, he realized that he'd learned a lesson after all—you don't have to be perfect, you just had to do the job. Was that the lesson Marti had in mind?

"Lucky you're skinny," Ryle said, looking down at him. "You missed getting splattered by an inch."

"Half an inch," Wyatt said.

He smiled, and for a half second, she smiled back. Then she shook her head briskly and walked over to the littles hovering in a corner. Vash hugged her hard.

"Bruh, you get to tell Marti," Diesel said and smirked at him, "how a stranded totally saved your butt."

"She wouldn't have had to"—Wyatt felt a white-hot coal of anger burn his gut—"if you hadn't left me hanging."

Wyatt wanted to throttle Diesel, but he couldn't shake the words "Marti wants to teach you a lesson." Was that true? Marti was hard on everyone, but she wasn't vicious. The jerk had to be lying. But what if he wasn't?

"Should've seen your face." Diesel clapped Wyatt on the shoulder. "Looked like you stained your whitey tighties."

Diesel had almost got him killed, and now it was no big deal? "Yeah, classic," Wyatt said, faking a smile.

"Lighten up, bruh. I'd never let you die."

Wyatt wasn't so sure. Diesel was a second-wave rider. He'd joined the train after they'd picked up him and Festus near Aurora station. Diesel had immediately wormed his way into the Council's good graces, before his true colors came out. By then, it was too late to exile him.

Diesel stared at Ryle, licking his lips, reminding Wyatt of a hungry zombie. "Hey! The new girl's been bit! Purge her before she turns!"

Ryle looked ruined. Her face drained of color, and her

eyes met Wyatt's. "But you said Cheddar could . . . that it's not the way we turn. . . ." She grabbed Wyatt's arm and whispered, "Who's going to watch over my littles?"

"You are," Wyatt said. "Because you're not turning."

She stuffed both hands into her back pockets, probably to hide her fear. But she couldn't keep it from her voice. "I'm really not?"

He watched the emotions cascade across her face. Worry. Panic. Betrayal. It was all there. After she'd gotten the Dumpty off the switch, he'd been so embarrassed. But now watching her work through the fear, he wanted her to be okay.

"It's not like the movies," he said. How could a survivor not know that? How long had she been on the run? Her clothes were new. Her hands were calloused but clean, and she had no apparent battle scars. Something wasn't adding up. He looked at Diesel. "Knock it off, or it's latrine duty."

Diesel snorted. "Only the conductor passes out punishments, little brother."

"News flash," Wyatt said. "Second-in-command passes out punishments. But you wouldn't know that since you're fifth in line."

Diesel grinned, and it was ugly. "Fourth ain't far away from second, know what I'm saying?"

Wyatt wanted to thump him, but he took a cleansing breath, like Pike had taught him. "Sounds like a threat to me. Something you want to say?" He tried to sound tough. That always worked for Pike.

Diesel punched Wyatt's arm. "Had you going, didn't I? You should've capped that Dumpty in the first place. Like Marti says, little zombie problems turn into big zombie problems." He turned to Ryle. "Don't get comfortable. We ain't taking no more hitchhikers."

"They stay till we clear Denver," Wyatt said.

"Marti decides on new riders." Diesel flicked his bangs off his forehead. "Ain't your decision to make."

"I made it, and if you don't like it, take it up with the conductor."

Diesel nodded. "My thoughts exactly. Festus! Let's go!"

He swung from the boxcar, then climbed the ladder topside. His heavy boots rang out as he ran across the top of the car.

Seconds later Festus pitter-pattered after him. "Wait up, Big D!"

"Is that Diesel dude for real?" Ryle said.

"A legend in his own mind," Wyatt said. "Let's see that bite again. Whoa. The zombie fresh got you good."

"Zombie fresh," Ryle said. "You keep using that word."

"Zombie fresh is what we call a zombie that's fresh turned."

"We call them rotters or the dead. They're the ones that can pass on the virus."

"They're not dead, just sick," Wyatt said, frowning. The wound had gotten dirty, and the skin was already puffy. It might kill her if it got infected. "It's a parasite, not a virus. Ask Cheddar. He'll explain it down to the tiniest detail. He likes details."

"You don't?"

Wyatt shrugged. Explanations had their own pitfalls. He'd rather say too little than too much. He rolled her sleeve down. "It's bleeding again. Put pressure on it."

"How long?"

"Till Cheddar says."

"No," she said. "How long before Marti kicks us off?"

"Not till it's safe."

"Define 'safe.'"

He avoided her gaze. "I promised you food, and I keep my promises."

Which meant he had to do the only thing more difficult and dangerous than dancing with a zombie fresh—convince Marti to let them stay.

7

WYATT

The map room was a converted baggage car. Almost a year before, Wyatt had helped Kendra and Pike replace the luggage racks with a scavenged leather pit group and four matching recliners. It was for Council meetings only. But when Marti became conductor, she made it her personal office.

Though it was only three-thirty p.m., the car was pitch-dark and smelled musty. The windows on the right side were covered with plywood papered with dozens of maps, the largest a pull-down of the Rockies. Lucille's route was traced in green and yellow highlighter. Short stretches were marked red. Black Xs dotted the track. Wyatt noticed a couple more had been added to the Union Pacific North Yard.

"Knock, knock," Wyatt said as he and Ryle entered. His hands shook. He tried to hide them behind his back. Why was he so nervous?

"Who's there?" Marti said.

"Wyatt. You know, *why you at* my house?"

Ryle smirked, but Marti scowled. So much for trying to lighten the mood.

"That joke wasn't funny when your brother used it."

Marti stood by the map, black marker in her fist. "And it's really not funny now."

Her eyes were locked on the town the train was headed for, Berkley, a suburb northwest of downtown Denver. Ten miles and two hours from the North Railyard. She drew a circle around it, then made hash marks to the east.

"Hate to interrupt your mapping," Ryle said, "but my kids are hungry."

Wyatt winced. Marti had a thing about disturbing—and disrespecting—the conductor.

Marti slowly turned. She'd lost a leg fighting off hijackers and wore a prosthetic. Her pants were rolled up to display it proudly. She was stout and short, with box braids. She carried a bokken practice sword, like a road warrior ready to take on the wasteland.

Wyatt was glad she was on his side, though he wondered if she still was after his epic screwup. "This is—"

Marti pointed the bokken at Ryle. "You're trespassing on my train."

"Ease off." Ryle glanced at Wyatt, a hint of mischief in her smile. "Didn't mean to start us off on the wrong foot."

"Was that a leg joke?" Marti said. "Because I don't have a sense of humor."

"It's true, she doesn't," Wyatt said and saw Ryle smirk. It had definitely been a jab. He admired Ryle's guts but not her lack of self-preservation.

"This is how you treat guests?" Ryle seemed unfazed. "We've survived out there a long time. Seen lots of bad kids gone feral who've forgotten how to be people."

"No bad people on my train," Marti said over the clack-clack of the wheels. Her body swayed as Lucille took a wide turn. "Only good ones."

"Your train," Ryle said, nodding like Marti had confirmed a suspicion. "Where'd you find it?"

"Back in the Union Pacific North Yard," Wyatt answered. "Right after the outbreak."

They had put the train together. It had been a group effort—him, Cheddar, Tuna, Pike, and the original members of the Council. And of course Pez, the engineer, who got Lucille started in the first place and kept her running now.

Marti cut Wyatt a harsh look. "Let's get this straight, trespasser. I ask the questions."

"We're not trespassing," Ryle said. "Wyatt invited us."

"Brakeman?" Marti said, cocking her head in disbelief.

Wyatt shrugged. "They did us a solid."

"We don't take hitchhikers, Brakeman. Did you forget the rule?"

"No, but—"

Wyatt felt a pang of conscience. When Kendra, Ricky, and Pike had made the rule, they hadn't wanted to exclude new riders. They wanted them to be trustworthy. Their mission was to run the circle till they found a survivor with immunity. How could they fulfill it by excluding strandeds?

"We've got more to fear from you than you from us, Conductor," Ryle said.

Marti shrugged like Ryle didn't bother her. But Wyatt knew questioning Marti's authority was as dangerous as whizzing on an electric fence.

"Tell me your story," Marti said, gesturing at Ryle with the bokken. "Make it good."

Ryle explained who they were and how they'd survived by scavenging what was left in upscale stores. When she finished, Marti sheathed the bokken, and Wyatt let out the breath he hadn't realized he'd been holding.

"That's all fine and good for the wasteland," Marti finally said. "But this is the zombie train."

They fell silent, and the smell of a decaying, burnt-out city seeped into the map car. Too bad Ryle hadn't boarded when Pike was still conducting. She'd make a great Council member. Watching her stand up to Marti made him want to push back against Marti, too.

"After the outbreak," Marti said, "survivors needed necessities. Food. Shelter. Medicine. Older kids demanded more. Answers. They wanted to know what caused the outbreak. How to cure it. Mostly they wanted to blame someone. Like finding out who'd caused their misery would make it hurt less. It took about ten days for the train's food supply to run out. Sickness spread. The older kids turned to zombies. That's when Pike and Kendra formed the Council, and the rest was history."

"Thanks for the lesson I didn't ask for, but does my crew get fed or not?" Ryle said, her stomach growling. "That's all I want to know."

Marti held up a hand to silence her. "I got problems, and more people means more problems. Here's the deal. You can join us, but a rider has to vouch for you. Somebody willing to lay down their life if you screw up."

"'Lay down their life'?" Ryle said. "Sounds like a line from a bad movie."

"The vouching rider offers their life as collateral," Marti said, ignoring her. "Any new rider that screws up, they get tossed off the train. The voucher gets purged, too."

"For real? That's ignorant," Ryle said, challenging Marti with a stare. "Nobody's going to vouch for six strandeds they just met. Nobody cares about us but us."

Footsteps pounded across the roof of the car. Ryle glanced at Wyatt. It was clear she knew he wouldn't take her side against the conductor. Yet that's exactly what his heart wanted to do. His brain, however, told him to follow orders.

"Keep your train," Ryle said. "We were doing fine without your 'hospitality.'"

Speak up, Wyatt chided himself. Take a stand. "Come on, Marti. Ryle got the Dumpty off the switch. Without her, Lucille would be halfway to Kansas."

Marti's eyebrows shot up, and her nostrils flared. "Whose fault is that, brakeman? You had one job—get a Dumpty off the switch, and you failed. Failures don't deserve to be my second. I'd promote Cheddar to number two, but he screwed up, too, and you know what happened to four."

"What?" Wyatt asked, his heart stopping. Tuna. What happened to Tuna? Then he remembered Marti saying something about trouble in the caboose. Trouble meant that a kid had started to turn. "What about Tuna?"

"That's train business," Marti said, "which we don't discuss with strandeds." She turned to Ryle. "Watch your back out there in the wild."

She held out a fist to bump, and Ryle ignored it.

"I'm a good zombie fighter," Ryle said. "You could've used me."

Ryle wasn't just a good zombie fighter. She was a great zombie fighter, better even than Pike. Mad quick. Fierce.

"Maybe," Marti said. "But now we'll never know."

"Yes, we will." Wyatt stepped up. The zombie train would be safer with Ryle on it. "I vouch for Ryle and her littles, and if I'm wrong about them, I'm willing to pay the price."

8

WYATT

"Have you lost your nose-picking mind?" Marti hissed minutes later.

More like I found it, Wyatt thought. After Wyatt's vow to vouch for Ryle and her crew, Marti had sent Ryle to the next car. When the door had closed behind her, Wyatt had turned back to Marti and met her hard stare.

"Our mission's to find a cure," he said. "How's that make me out of my mind?"

"Who replaces me?" Marti demanded.

"I do."

"Who replaces you?"

"Cheddar."

"And Cheddar?"

"Tuna, then Diesel." But only if we're desperate, Wyatt thought. Diesel was so far down the pecking order, it'd take an epic disaster to promote him. "What's your point?"

"Putting your life on the line for strandeds, it's not only your neck at risk. It's every kid who has to take your place. Bet you hadn't thought of that."

He had thought about it. It'd sat heavy on his mind since he took Ricky's place on the Council. Knowing the consequences didn't change his mind. Strandeds weren't a danger to Lucille. They were her lifeblood—especially the littles. One kid might be immune. The survivor they were searching for. It was worth the risk.

"Marti, I made up my mind before I opened my mouth."

"And you still did something stupid?" Marti scoffed. "Maybe Diesel didn't teach you that lesson."

"What? Diesel wasn't full of it?"

She clicked her tongue. "Diesel knows how to follow orders."

Diesel knows how to suck up. Then he remembered something he needed to ask. "Marti," he said. "Where's Tuna?"

"You know what happens in the caboose."

Like Cheddar, Tuna was a year younger than Wyatt, although they were in the same grade. Tuna had started reading early, so they'd placed him into first grade instead of kindergarten. His deliberate way of walking made him a social outcast, so his parents refused to let him skip more grades. It didn't help much. Then in middle school, he met Wyatt and Cheddar, and they were inseparable even after the zombies came.

"Marti, where is Tuna?"

He had to hear the truth, no matter how much it hurt. It had been that way with Pike, too, when it had felt like Wyatt's heart had been ripped out. At least his brother had delivered the news himself.

Marti pursed her lips, and for a half second, there was a

crack in her mask. She looked at the map wall, as if search-ing for something. "It happens to the best of us. The worst, too."

Tuna's six months younger than me, Wyatt thought. Now I'm the oldest boy in the world. That meant that he was overdue, a realization that hit him like a shockwave. When it dissipated, he was left with one thought. Once it's my time to conduct, I'll be ready.

He looked up, and Marti's mask was back.

"Suck it up, brakeman," she said. "There's no crying on the zombie train."

9

RYLE

When Wyatt opened the door to the infirmary car, Ryle saw that the windows sparkled, and the floors had been scrubbed. The air smelled of pine cleaner and cheeriness. Then she saw crayon drawings taped all over the windows. People. Houses. Dogs and cats. Lots of families, especially. Not a single zombie anywhere. She felt a tug of sadness for a world that was no more.

It had only been a few minutes since the meeting with Marti, but Ryle was anxious to see the rest of the train. "What's this car?"

"This is the infirmary car," he said and let her go first, like chivalry still mattered.

Wyatt was a nice kid. Nice got you hurt. "You vouched for us?" Ryle said as they walked toward the back. This car had windows from floor to ceiling. So much brighter than the dingy map car. Outside, she could see signs for I-76 and Pecos Junction. "Does that mean we're free to move about?"

"There'll be a ceremony later, but yeah, you can. Now, let's get that wound patched up." He opened one of the compartment doors. "This old Superliner car had fourteen sleeping compartments, but we repurposed four. Cheddar needed storage for medicine, bandages, crutches. Plus an examination room."

He hit the lights.

"Electricity?" she gasped. She had almost forgotten it existed.

"The engine is also a generator." He smiled and closed the door. "We've got air-conditioning and heat, too."

"Sweet," she said. "Sleeper compartments are only for patients?"

"Oh no, we all get a compartment in the sleeping cars. Ten-and-unders have to share, but elevens and twelves get their own space. You'll get one, too, after the vouching."

"Seriously?" No wonder Parcheesi wanted the train. "You're not getting my hopes up?"

He laughed, the first time she could remember. He seemed so different from the kid who couldn't hurt a glob zombie.

"Don't worry, the train is like a big family." He gestured for her to follow. "Cheddar's waiting."

When they reached the examination room, Cheddar was sitting at a table. Vash sat opposite him, playing with a roll of surgical tape. The table was covered with bandages, antibiotics, and ointment. Ryle was irritated that Vash hadn't found the engineer and made friends, but she held her tongue.

In the infirmary the heat was running, and it was so toasty, Ryle felt drowsy. They'd spent months in cold box-cars, and the warmth felt like a blanket.

Wyatt gave Ryle the thumbs-up. "Take care of her, Ched."

"Why would I not?" Cheddar said, tilting his head.

"Only an expression. Don't be so literal."

"This way, then." Cheddar led Ryle to the sink and gently rinsed her wound. "I'm irrigating the bite," he said, "to wash out the bacteria. Now have a seat."

"Looks like y'all cleaned out the medicine cabinet for me." Ryle slid next to Vash, gave her an exploding fist bump, and looked up at Wyatt. "You're not sitting?"

Wyatt shook his head. "Ched gets hinky when I butt in."

"That's why y'all are friends," Vash said. "'Cause you respect his space?"

"That, and he was the one who saved me after our biology teacher, Mrs. Ramirez, turned into Mrs. Zombirez, and we escaped the school ahead of a line of bloodsucking cafeteria ladies."

"I only hit the fire alarm. Wy is the one who sprayed her with a fire extinguisher." Cheddar blushed and rolled up Ryle's sleeve. "Also." He gestured around. "This isn't the whole medicine cabinet. We salvaged a Cheyenne medical clinic two loops ago, and we are equipped to treat almost any illness. This is going to sting."

"Ow!" Ryle winced as Cheddar squirted antiseptic into the wound. "You said sting, not burn like fire."

"Dang, girl." Vash sucked air between her teeth and patted Ryle's shoulder. "That zombie chomped you like a chew toy."

"It was so fast, Vash," Ryle said. "You're sure I'm not going to turn, Cheddar?"

"You'll definitely turn," Cheddar said, then paused when Vash gasped. "But not from this bite. The change is caused by a parasite that only affects adults."

"But everybody knows—" Ryle began.

"Everything you know about zombies is wrong," Cheddar said.

She glanced at Wyatt, who was barely hiding a smirk. "Cheddar, was your daddy a doctor?"

"My mom was a pediatric infectious disease researcher at CU med school. My dad was an ER nurse and an amateur chef."

"You learned first aid from the ER, then?"

He laughed. "From my dad's cooking lessons. You would be surprised how spatchcocking a chicken prepares you for minor surgery." Cheddar reached for a bandage. "Also, chefs are infamous for cuts and burns."

"What'd you get from your mama?" Vash said, passing him the scissors. "Your smooth-talking charm?"

"A stack of medical textbooks and the capacity to use them." He swatted Ryle's hand when she tried to touch the wound. "I'll change the dressing in a few hours. Keep it dry, please."

"I'll do my best." Ryle stood and looked up at Wyatt. She wasn't used to looking up to anybody. "My kids are safe?"

"Safer than safe," Wyatt said. "Tater fetched canned milk and cookies after their baths. I bet they've eaten twice their weight in Oreos."

Oreos? They had cookies! Medicine, food, a safe place to sleep, and cookies. And a brakeman who used words like fetch. Who even talked like that? She felt a flutter of hope, then tamped it down. Hope could get you killed.

"Can I get some of that?" Vash said, looking out the window as the train went around a sharp bend, and the yellow-and-black locomotive came into full view.

"Milk and cookies?" Wyatt said.

"No, that!" She pointed at Lucille. "I always wanted to see a train engine for real."

Way to get back on point, Ryle thought. Maybe Vash had been waiting for the right opportunity.

"Our engineer loves company." Wyatt moved to the center of the car and pulled down a trapdoor in the ceiling. "Follow me."

But Vash wasn't following anybody. She climbed

through the trapdoor and pulled herself atop of the car. "Move your butt, Ryle! We can run the cars, just like the movies!"

Then she took off.

"Sorry," Ryle said to Wyatt. "We're working on her impulse control."

Wyatt shrugged and held the trapdoor open. "No problem. We travel on the cars more than through them. After you?"

The sun was dropping behind the Rockies' Front Range, and the evening sky was a dusky purple stain, reflecting off cotton candy wisps of clouds. It felt like the temp was dropping outside as they passed signs for Berkley, then Westminster as the train tracked northwest.

Ryle climbed up, then ran along the top before jumping to the next car, following Vash. She landed hard, jarring her arm, and she felt a snap of pain where the zombie had bit her. If it really was only a bite. But if she were going to turn, she would've by now, right? Parcheesi was definitely wrong. And if she was wrong about bites, what else was she wrong about? Ryle needed some time alone to sort things out, but it'd have to wait till she was squirreled away in the room Wyatt had promised. Until then, she'd play the game.

Vash was waiting impatiently at the cab door when Ryle and Wyatt got there. "Hurry! I've got to see this engine!"

She bounced like a little needing to go potty. "It's like Christmas morning!"

Vash's excited puppy act was over the top, but Wyatt was eating it up. If Ryle didn't know better, she would've believed her, too.

"My granddaddy," Vash explained as Wyatt opened the door and led them down the cramped space between the boilers and the control box, "he kept a track in the basement. I'd sneak down at night and run the trains together. Boom!"

The narrow hallway was loud, and they were surrounded by engines, huge steamy pipes, moving pistons, and diesel vapors that burned Ryle's nose.

"Watch your mouth around Lucille." A lanky boy stepped away from the control box. His face was covered with soot and grease. "She's sensitive."

"Don't scare me like that!" Vash yelled and swatted him. "I might hit you accidentally on purpose."

The engineer recoiled, fiddling with the straps on his overalls, which were so stained with grease, he looked like a part of the engine. He smelled of burnt fuel, sweat, and awkwardness.

"They talk about the train," Ryle whispered to Vash, "like it's a person."

She understood immediately why Pez wore no shirt. It was brutally hot in the locomotive, literally boiling, as the pressure gauges showed. She lifted her hair to cool her neck and realized that her shirt was already soaked. She felt a tiny bit of sympathy for Vash, who had to learn to run this monster of a machine.

Wyatt pulled the lanky boy back over to Vash. "This is Pez, our engineer," he said. "He keeps Lucille moving. Pez, this is Ryle and Vash."

"Hello, Pez." Ryle felt sorry for the poor kid. His hands were shaking, and he couldn't make eye contact. "Nice to—"

Pez ignored her extended hand. "Boss, about engine two."

"That's not a hello, Pez," Wyatt said.

Pez fiddled with his overalls and glared at Vash. "What kind of monster crashes model trains?"

"A bored monster, that's who," Vash said. "You never crashed nothing?"

"Don't say *crash* around Lucille," Pez said. "She's the nervous type."

"I just did," Vash said. "Crash!"

Pez put his fingers in his ears. "Lalala! I can't hear you!" He ducked back behind the control board. "Lalala!"

Vash followed on his heels. "Crash! Boom! Bang!"

"Vash, leave him alone." Ryle turned back to Wyatt. "She gets hyper sometimes. Most times. Well, all the time."

"Pez could use some hyper," Wyatt said. "He spends too much time with his dials and gauges. Want a tour of the train?"

Absolutely, she did. Her job was to learn about everything—fuel, supplies, riders, and weapons. She had to play it cool, so they wouldn't suspect anything. "I already saw the infirmary and the map car. What else is there?"

"There's more to this train than meets the eye," he said. The longer he was away from Marti, the more confident he sounded. Maybe Ryle had misjudged him.

"What about Pez?" she said. "Vash can be like a road-runner on Red Bull."

They glanced into the cab. The loud voices had died down, and Pez was talking calmly. "But my gramps had done died, and I got to run a locomotive without nobody saying it'd take years of schooling."

Vash reached for the throttle, and Pez blocked her hand. "Lucille's fussy about who touches her."

"Then we'll wait," Vash said, "till she knows me better."

"But she won't mind if you blow the horn," he said, pointing to a string running above them.

Vash grinned and pulled the line. Lucille let out a long blast, and Vash practically giggled. Maybe she wasn't faking the joy.

Ryle shrugged. "Okay, I don't *think* Vash will break anything."

"Love at first sight," Wyatt said, heading toward the door. "This way, ma'am."

"You're calling me 'ma'am'?" Ryle laughed. "That's wild."

"You can't get wilder than a zombie apocalypse."

Want to bet? Ryle thought. Wait till you see who's waiting on the tracks ahead.

10

RYLE

Everything is so neat, Ryle thought as they entered the sightseer car. Like a Mr. Clean commercial. She kept waiting for the surfaces to twinkle. One side of the car was decorated with birthday cards taped to the windows. Last year Ryle had celebrated her eleventh birthday in the wilderness with a Twinkie and a single candle that wouldn't light.

"This is our sightseer observation car." Wyatt gestured out the floor-to-ceiling windows to the ash-cocooned Denver high-rises, overshadowed by the golden spire of the Cash Register Building. "Good place to sit and think. Tater only lets little ones up here for story time."

"Tater?"

"Chief cook and bottle washer. He's in charge of the littles. Feeds them, reads them stories . . . "

Ryle watched the husks of distant skyscrapers eek by. Why did they run the locomotive so slowly? Any determined zombie could jump on. "So this Tater," she said. "He's good with kids?"

"Tater?" Wyatt laughed. "He hates them."

"Then why's he in charge?"

"'Cause he's a control freak who kept bossing us around,

so the Council gave him the job."

"The Council?"

Wyatt pointed down the sightseer car's center aisle. "Dining car's that way."

The dining car smelled like tomato soup and grilled cheese. Ryle's stomach rumbled. She'd been living off Vienna sausages and dry cereal for the last few weeks, and her belly had ideas.

"Howdy, y'all," Wyatt said.

A couple dozen kids looked up. They were from fourish to tenish. Coloring books. Crayons. Paints. Comics. Wyatt greeted them with high fives, and they grinned back. She hadn't seen that many smiles in forever.

"Where's my crew?" she asked.

Wyatt pointed to the rear of the car. "Being kids."

She followed him down the aisle. In the back booths, her four kids slurped down tomato soup like it was candy. "Wow," she said. "They're behaving themselves."

"Tater's soup does that." He patted a short kid's shoulder. His black hair was cut straight across his forehead, and the look on his face was a sour as a Lemonhead. "Ryle, this is Tater."

"Then the kids must be Tater tots," Ryle said and grinned.

Tater drew back like he'd licked a rancid chicken. "Har. Har. Always the same pun. I don't like puns."

"If I can't call them Tater tots," Ryle said, "how about small fry?"

"You're vouching for them?" Tater growled at Wyatt. "Because that's six more hungry mouths. This ain't no restaurant."

Whoa, Ryle thought. Definitely not a nurturer. But useful. When they took over the train, they would let him stay—if he behaved. "My tots will do their share. Don't worry."

"Do I look worried?" Tater threw a dish towel over his shoulder. "Leroy! Ginny! Clean up! Show the newbies how it's done."

He disappeared into the galley. Ginny and Leroy put their books down and collected the dishes. It looked like every rider had a job, and they got it done without being asked twice. No complaining and no threats. Impressive.

"So how many cars on the train?" she asked.

"Twelve. Fuel car, map car, sightseer lounge, dining car, infirmary, three sleepers, two boxcars, a flatcar, and the caboose."

"Nice," Ryle said. If the end of the train was storage, that's where it was vulnerable. "Why couldn't we get on the caboose before?"

He shrugged.

Okay, mister. Keep your secrets. For now. "Is that all the kids do?" she asked as they exited the car. "Eat Oreos and draw?"

"Tater keeps them busy," he said. "There's story time every night. Every third day is game night, and every fourth is movie night. They do school stuff in the mornings."

"What's the point of school?"

"We all said the same thing when our first conductor, Kendra, started the school. Till she pointed out the truth."

"What's that?"

"We used to learn to make our own lives better. Now we're learning to make all our lives better. To keep the human race going till we find a cure."

A shiver went down Ryle's spine. A cure. Wyatt acted like he believed it actually existed. Stupid. Maybe it wouldn't take force to execute Parcheesi's plan. Maybe with the right words, Wyatt could be convinced. If only Marti wasn't the conductor.

They walked through the next car, Cheddar's infirmary car. This time, Ryle spotted a compartment labeled DO NOT ENTER.

She tapped the door. "What's in here?"

"A . . . medical library. Cheddar's, um, very protective of his books."

Was it her imagination or did Wyatt turn a little pale? He was obviously hiding something. "Can we go in? Promise I won't touch anything."

He shook his head and kept walking. "The next three cars are sleepers, but we converted the last one to put in storage lockers for the paintball armory and our cannon."

She followed him inside. "You have a real cannon?"

"It's a water cannon."

Ryle wondered what other weapons they had in the armory. "You fight zombie herds with paintballs and water?"

"We have little kids on the train," he said, leading her quickly through all three sleeper cars. "No guns, no swords. Too dangerous. Plus, one paintball to the eyes, and a zombie's useless."

He's lying.

He stopped at the end of the third and last sleeper coach and pointed out the vestibule window. "Lastly and leastly, we've got the boxcars for food and then the flatbed for storing vehicles. Dirt bikes for our scouts. ATVs. Water tanker. Then it's two boxcars for food, water, clothes, supplies. The usual. You saw all this when you got on, so our tour ends here."

Ryle pointed to six narrow compartments at the rear of the coach. They went from floor to ceiling, and they were made of steel. "What do you store in these?"

"Bad people."

"It's the jail?"

"Something like that."

Oh, so he was being evasive now. She felt a twinge of satisfaction. "How many prisoners have you taken?"

"Three." Wyatt tugged at his wristband and looked away from the cells. "We hope to never take another one. Now if you'd follow me back to—"

"What about the caboose?"

He shook his head. "We use it for storage."

"Storage," she repeated. He was lying through his teeth. It made her feel slightly less guilty for lying through hers.

Back in the first sleeper car, Wyatt unlocked the door to a compartment and gave Ryle the key. "This room's yours," he said. "Vash is across the hall, and your littles are in the second sleeper."

"Will they be safe?"

"Don't worry. There's always somebody standing watch."

He swung the door open and walked into the compartment. He pointed to an army footlocker by the bed. "Lock your valuables in there, and nobody will touch them."

"Valuables?" She snorted. "Like what?"

"Canned fruit, candy, chocolate. Spam is great for trading." He shrugged. "Make yourself at home. Have a nap. Take a shower."

"Shower?"

He pointed to a door. "Your private bath. Sink, toilet, shower. Try to keep showers short. Hot water runs out fast."

"Did you say hot water?"

"It's chilly in here. Your thermostat is on that wall. Oh, yeah. I forgot."

He turned and left. She could hear his boots echo down the aisle. Then he was running back with a can of milk in one hand and a bag of Oreos in the other. "Saved some for you."

Have I died and gone to heaven? Ryle thought. "If you're trying to bribe me with cookies, it's working."

"Every rider gets their share." He handed them to her. "See you at dinner."

Ryle twisted an Oreo apart and scraped the filling off with her teeth. Oh, yeah, heaven. She flicked the thermostat to heat and felt the warm air blow on her face. She stepped into the cramped bathroom and flushed the toilet.

She giggled and flushed it again.

Toilet paper. There was actual toilet paper.

She stuffed another Oreo into her mouth and plopped onto the bed. The sky was purple with twilight when she spread her arms and legs like a snow angel and closed her eyes. Just to rest them.

Marti's voice broke over the PA, yanking Ryle from a sound sleep.

"All riders!" Marti said, sounding mad at the world. "Report to the helipad in ten minutes!"

Not me, Ryle thought, and lay back down. Her head felt

full of marshmallow puff. She hadn't slept that soundly in forever.

A knock.

She groaned and groggily answered the door. Wyatt was waiting.

"You've got a helipad to land helicopters," she asked, "and you didn't show me?"

Wyatt shrugged. "It's not really a helipad. It's just where we gather for the vouching. After this, you'll be one of us, and we'll show Marti it's okay to trust you."

"Yeah, well," she said. "I'll meet you there in a few." Then, she thought, we'll see who trusts who.

11

WYATT

Wyatt climbed onto the helipad, which was a simple white circle painted on top of the infirmary car. The sun was setting, and the temp had dropped maybe thirty degrees. Lucille was passing through Louisville, twenty-five miles northwest of Denver. The Union Pacific rails had been laid decades ago when the area was mostly ranchland. Now the city was so overdeveloped, it felt like they could touch the buildings on either side—a Mexican restaurant and a clothing store—as they passed.

Wyatt didn't know what reception he'd get from Marti. He was done with trying to please her. "You rang, conductor?"

Marti turned slowly, the day's dying light reflecting like a halo off her braids. She reached for the hilt of her bokken, and Wyatt knew he was in deep trouble. Then she smiled and stuck out her hand. He couldn't keep the surprise off his face, but he took her hand and endured the bone-crushing shake.

"You're right," she said. "It's not my job to keep outsiders off the train. It's not what Kendra would want."

Wyatt felt his head spin, baffled by her sudden change of heart.

"If I stepped down as conductor," she said, "could you do the job? Are you up to that challenge?"

He didn't hesitate. "I am."

She shook her head. "You're never going to be Pike, but when I'm gone, you might make a tolerable conductor."

"Thanks. I . . . " Words abandoned him again. She'd been showing tough love. She really did believe in him.

"Which is why," she said, "I'm promoting Diesel to brakeman and adding Tater to the Council as number four. You'll be number five."

"Five?" Her words roared in his ears. She had gotten his hopes up so she could crush them! "You're demoting me?"

She dusted off his shoulders. "Think of it as time to grow into the job. If you live long enough."

"I'm older than Diesel and Tater. I'll turn before I become conductor."

Marti shrugged. "C'est la vie."

"No, I'm not Pike or Kendra." His words caught in his throat. "But I'm next up, and you can't take that away."

"The conductor chooses the Council," she said, crossing her arms like a smug pirate. "Look, I'm doing you a favor. Trust me. You're *not* ready."

Before Wyatt could argue, the riders started arriving, their heads popping up as they climbed the ladders on either end of the car. They gathered around the circular helipad, then Ryle and her crew joined them.

"This isn't over," Wyatt said under his breath.

"Riders!" Marti stepped into the bull's-eye and waited for silence. "Strangers wish to join us, and someone must vouch for their loyalty." She stared at Wyatt. "For if a new rider violates train rules, they'll be purged, and so will the voucher."

Wyatt flinched. His neck was on the line.

"Strandeds, come forward!"

The littles lined up shoulder to shoulder, Vash on one end and Ryle on the other. With the twilight sun casting orange light on their faces, they waited as Marti rested her hands on Vash's head.

"Who vouches for this one?" Marti called out.

Wyatt stepped into the circle, spine as straight and rigid as steel. "I do."

"Done." Marti moved on. "Who vouches?"

"I do," his voice rang out.

Marti moved on, and Wyatt's voice got louder and stronger each time. A murmur swept through the riders. Maybe they thought he was stupid to take the risk.

Marti reached up to touch Ryle's head. "Who vouches?"

Wyatt met Ryle's eyes. What was she thinking? Was it a mistake risking his life for her? Only a fool would do it.

"I vouch," he said.

A cheer went up around the circle. The riders all rushed in, showering the new riders with hugs and back slaps and cheers.

Ryle looked overwhelmed, and Wyatt thought she might panic and bolt. Then a little boy wrapped his arms around Ryle's waist, and she wiped her eyes.

Wyatt looked away to a wooden fence that ran alongside the tracks, built to block the noise of the train. Behind it was a typical Denver suburb, with houses crammed all together, once full of families. Now it was as deserted as downtown, full of weeds and sagebrush—and—his eye caught movement, and his heart stopped. The neighborhood wasn't empty. The streets, the sidewalks, even the spaces between houses.

Shamblers.

"Son of a biscuit eater," he said and turned to Marti. "Are you seeing this?"

She came up beside him. "Gather the Council in the map room," she said. "Now. It's time for you to learn—oof."

Her words drained away. She put a hand over the arrow embedded in her heart, and when she pulled her hand away, it was drenched in blood.

12

RYLE

The temperature in Boulder had dropped below freezing when Ryle joined the Council in the map car. In the two hours since Marti had been shot, they'd locked down the train. On Wyatt's orders, Tater had doubled the guard. Nobody could tell where the arrow had come from. They had all hit the deck, waiting for more. But after three silent minutes, Wyatt had taken command. His first order was to send Vash and the littles downstairs. Then he directed Diesel, Tater, Ryle, and Cheddar to take Marti's body to a boxcar. They'd carried her between them, cringing and ducking the entire time, afraid they'd be shot next.

But no more arrows ever came.

"Welcome to Council, everyone," Wyatt said, calling the meeting to order. "First item of business is Marti. Maybe it was a random shot. Maybe it was ferals. There's no way of knowing, so we keep moving."

"Wait. Marti just died." Cheddar raised his hand. "The riders are in shock. They need closure."

"In the morning Marti will have a prairie burial," Wyatt said. "But the train doesn't stop."

Cheddar shook his head but didn't argue.

"Are you sure we're safe?" Ryle asked. "The archer could still be out there."

"The archer is out there," Wyatt said. "Nothing we can do about it, except keep rolling. Next order of business. Replacing a couple of Council members."

"You're acting like the conductor," Diesel said, "but we ain't voted, and I'm throwing my hat in the ring."

Tater gave Diesel the stink eye. "The brakeman becomes conductor when number one goes down," he said. "Now's not time for your mess, Diesel."

"It's time for my mess when I say it's time," Diesel said.

"Okay, let's have a vote," Wyatt said. "Cheddar?"

"All in favor of Diesel being conductor," Cheddar said, "raise your hand."

Diesel raised his hand.

"All those in favor of Wyatt?" Cheddar said.

Ryle raised her hand, along with Tater, Cheddar, and of course, Wyatt.

"Hey!" Diesel complained. "Ryle ain't allowed to vote. Neither's Tater."

"I already disregarded their votes," Cheddar said. "It's still two to one. Wyatt carries the day."

"Hurry it up," Tater said, yawning. "The rugrats will want breakfast in five hours."

"Yeah," Ryle said. "And he has to ketchup on his beauty sleep."

Tater glared at her. "It's too late for puns."

"Tired of my tater taunts?" Ryle said and smirked, but inside, she was relieved.

The stars were aligning. Marti had been the biggest hurdle, and in a snap, the hurdle had disappeared. She felt a pang of guilt. Get a grip, she told herself. It was a fluke, and now Wyatt was in charge, and he believed there was a zombie cure. She only had to convince him that she possessed it.

"We need to fill two Council seats," Wyatt said. "The conductor chooses the seats."

Ryle noticed that something about his eyes had changed. He was wearing the same clothes and the same gun belt on his hip. But he looked different.

Wyatt gave Cheddar a fist bump. "You're still number three."

Cheddar looked relieved. "So glad I'm not the brakeman. What a disaster that would be."

"Tater," Wyatt said, "you're number four."

Tater yawned. "Whatever."

"Diesel, you're off the Council." Wyatt turned stonefaced. "Leave the car."

"Dude! Seriously?" Diesel barked, looking like a bull about to charge.

"Dead serious." Wyatt drew his paintball gun. "You're leaving one way or another."

"Who you kidding?" Diesel said, practically spitting. "Paintballs can't stop me!"

Wyatt cocked an eyebrow. "Depends on where they hit."

Diesel's eyes widened. "You wouldn't dare!"

Ryle smiled. Brakeman Wyatt might not have made that threat, but Conductor Wyatt meant business.

"Y'all think you're safe 'cause you're buddies?" Diesel turned to the others. "Anybody draws a gun on a man will draw it on his friends."

"Stop quoting Pike," Cheddar said. "And you're not his friend."

"You're not a man, either," Tater said.

Diesel told them where they could stick it. Then he stomped toward the exit. "Bruh, you made a huge mistake. Huge!"

The door slammed behind him.

"Council needs new blood." Wyatt nodded to Ryle. "She's number two."

Ryle gasped. "You've got to be kidding."

"First thing in the morning," Wyatt said, "you start brake training."

Tater yawned, and Cheddar cracked his knuckles. Neither seemed concerned about Diesel's tantrum. But Ryle wondered if Wyatt really had made a huge mistake. Diesel seemed the vengeful type.

"I'm going to bed," Tater mumbled and headed for the exit.

"Me too," Cheddar said and followed him. "Funeral day tomorrow."

"You're not sleepy?" Wyatt asked Ryle.

"Can't wait to crawl into a warm bed," she said. "But putting me on Council? It might come back to haunt you."

"Diesel's all bark and no bite." He pointed at her arm. "By the way, how's your bite?"

Ryle tapped the bandage. "Cheddar changed the dressing."

"That's going to leave an ugly scar."

She shrugged. "Not like it's my only one."

Ryle pulled up her jeans to expose a jagged scar on her calf. "Got in a fight with a feral. Got me with a broken Coke bottle. One of the green ones."

Wyatt pulled up his shirt. There was a circle-shaped scar near his spine. "From a stranded we let on the train. Jabbed me with a stick."

Ryle lifted her shirt and tapped a puckered scar above her hip bone. "Mine's better."

Wyatt whistled. "Impressive. How did you get it?"

"Fell off a tree picking apples, straight onto a spiked metal fence. Sucker impaled me."

"Not an epic battle with a zombie lord?" he asked. "How did you get off the fence?"

"Oh, that. Par—my friends saved me. Don't know exactly how because I'd passed out. Probably should've died." She tucked in her shirt. "I win the scar competition, yeah?"

"Quality, yes. Quantity, no."

"Quality always beats quantity." She shook her head and pointed at the yellow band on his wrist. "What's on it?"

"It says, *Stand up*. My mom's favorite motto. She gave it to me."

"That's cool," Ryle said and suddenly wanted to change the subject. "I'm the brakeman? That means I ride the brakes like a granny?"

Wyatt laughed. "Brakeman's an outdated term. Modern locomotives have a control board that handles everything, so Pez doesn't need help. Basically, you do everything the conductor asks."

"Like cleaning zombies off tracks."

"Or recording routes on the maps," he said. "And communicating with Pez, which is the hardest job of all."

"You mean these maps?" Ryle traced a finger along the highlighted route. From Denver, it went north to Wyoming, west to Salt Lake City, south through Utah, then east back to Denver. One huge loop, like Parcheesi said. "Where did you find them?"

"My old school. Geography class."

"Smart." She traced the circle west back to Utah, and the phrase *if we can make Utah* popped into her head. Her finger stopped at Salt Lake, where a rail line turned northwest. Perfect. All the way to Puget Sound.

"My geography teacher, Mrs. Garcia, collected old maps," he said. "When the grid went down, I knew we'd need to navigate, so we went back to school to grab some."

"We?"

"Me, my big brother, Cheddar, and some other friends."

"Where's your brother now?"

"Turned."

"Oh," Ryle said, feeling like a complete fool. Big brother. Of course he would've turned. "I'm sorry."

"It happens," he said. "Anyway, that loop you're tracing? We've done it fourteen times. A thousand miles and change every time."

"How long does it take?"

"A week or two. Depends on if we have to clear track. Longer if we run into avalanches or landslides. They're bad in the canyons between Granby and Grand Junction."

"What are the black marks for?"

"Points where zombies congregate. Like here." He tapped the border between Colorado and Kansas. "Massive herds on the eastern plains. They could stop the train, so we will never go that way."

"What about the red crosses?"

He hesitated for a second. "Prairie burials."

"Wyatt!" Festus dropped from the hatch atop the car, landing behind Ryle. "Diesel said to—"

Ryle whirled and drew her bō. She stuck the metal tip under Festus' knobby chin. "Never. Sneak. Up. On. Me."

"Conductor!" Festus' tiny Adam's apple bobbed perilously close to the steel. "Don't let her whomp me!"

"Don't be so melodramatic," Ryle said, then smirked, but she held back the staff. She wasn't one to make showy threats. But sometimes you had to do things you didn't like.

Festus scratched his head. "Melo-dra-what?"

"What do you want, Festus?" Wyatt demanded.

"Nurse said there was a . . . um . . . bad coupling on the caboose."

"Tell the nurse I'll be there in a minute."

"Okay, but Big D says it's a 911-type emergency," Festus said, then jumped to the hatch and disappeared.

"Impressive," Ryle said. "Is he part subway rat?"

"Just looks like one. But he's as quiet as he is quick, and you never hear him coming."

"Why put up with him and Diesel if they cause problems?"

"We learned the hard way not to throw people off the train." Wyatt glanced at the map again. This time at a red X in Cheyenne. "It comes back to bite you."

Ryle locked the hatch. "So do rats."

"Festus isn't so bad. All he really wants is friends." Wyatt checked his gun and loaded it with paintballs. "He just picked a bad one. Back soon."

Ryle smirked. It wasn't loaded before. Diesel got played. She had to give it to Wyatt. It was a pretty good bluff. As he left, she wondered if she'd seriously underestimated him. Then something hit her. Who was the nurse, and why hadn't she met this person?

13

WYATT

Minutes later Wyatt entered the caboose vestibule, a small room lit by a dim overhead bulb, separated from the cabin by a thick oak door. A bloodred door. His breath freezing in the air, he unlocked a footlocker and pulled out body armor and a motorcycle helmet, then unclipped a gaff from a wall bracket.

He paced the vestibule, trying to make the puzzle pieces fit together. Marti had been shot standing right beside him. The arrow could've hit him. But in the blink of an eye, he was the conductor. Life was so random. Yesterday he thought conducting was the plum job, but already it was the hardest thing he'd done in his life—except for sending his own brother to the caboose.

Do the job, he thought, and knocked on the red door. "It's Wyatt. Open up."

A viewing slot slid open. "What took so long?" the nurse said, face hidden in shadow. "Where's the conductor? And where's your coat?"

"I'm the conductor now," Wyatt said. "Festus said one's about to turn. Was he lying?"

"Not this time."

"That fast?"

"Some kids go that fast."

"Is it—"

The nurse swung the door open. "Not yet."

The caboose had been retrofitted with chains from a large animal vet's office bolted to the walls. Cages installed. Pike and the Council had built it early on to contain riders as they turned.

One by one, everyone found themselves in the caboose.

Wyatt carefully walked past the cages. Inside, kids screamed in raw, feral voices. It wasn't the volume that raised his hackles. It was the intensity.

"Fresh meat gets their blood up," the nurse said. "Don't let it bother you."

"Easy for you to say," Wyatt said. "You're not the fresh meat."

"Nothing's easy for me to say."

Wyatt fixed his eyes straight ahead. He'd seen thousands of zombies. Right after the outbreak, every grown-up was zombie fresh. Fast. Ravenous. Ready to eat anything it could sink its teeth into. These were different. They were train people. Friends.

The nurse stopped at the last cell and opened a small viewing door. A savage face with bloody red eyes slammed into the gap. Spittle flew, and broken teeth gnashed the cage bars.

"Kendra?" Wyatt exhaled disappointment. "Thought

she might make it, she lasted so long."

"They all look like they might beat the parasite. Right up to the very end."

Wyatt adjusted the chin strap on his helmet and dropped the visor. He leveled the gaff. If he missed the limbic cortex, the lizard part of the brain, he'd have to do it again and again.

He waited until her jerking subsided, then rammed the sharp point through.

"Good termination," the nurse said. "It was kind."

Good termination. Wyatt hated the praise. This had always been his job. Not the brakeman's. Not the conductor's. His and his alone. He propped the gaff against the wall. "I've had too much practice."

The nurse opened the cage and carried Kendra out. Not Kendra—the zombie she'd become. Just an empty husk. Thinking that way made the job easier but did nothing for the nightmares.

The nurse carried Kendra to the rear platform and put her down gently. Wyatt said a prayer. Then they pushed the body off. It hit the embankment and rolled into the tall overgrowth. A prairie burial in a sea of grass.

The nurse locked the door. "How many is that?"

"Eleven."

"It never gets any easier?"

"Just faster," Wyatt said softly.

They walked back through the caboose, and a ruckus broke out. From inside the cages, human voices called out his name.

"Still don't know how you stand the noise." Wyatt covered his ears. "I'd never get used to it."

"It has to be done," the nurse said. "Who else is there?"

Wyatt nodded to acknowledge the sacrifice. Without the nurse, they would have to exile their friends as soon as they showed the first signs of turning—red eyes, hair loss, black fingernails. They'd never know who was immune and who wasn't. So far, everyone had completely fallen to the parasite, except the nurse. That gave Wyatt hope for a cure, but the hope was fading.

"Any others close to quarantine?" the nurse said.

Ryle, Wyatt thought. She was about his age, and that made her a senior citizen. "Nobody," he said, reaching for the door handle. Then he turned around.

"Tuna?"

Tuna stared through the bars of the cage closest to the door. His pupils dilated then shrank, dilated then shrank. If eyes were the windows to the soul, Tuna's soul was in purgatory. Human. Not human. Dead. Not dead.

Wyatt took two steps toward the cage. His fingers had almost reached the bars when a hand shot out, broken nails and gnawed fingers clawing the air.

"Tuna," he whispered. "I'm sorry."

"Sorry's for dead men." The nurse grabbed Wyatt by the collar. "You need to go."

"He recognizes me."

"Today he does."

Wyatt pulled off the helmet. He tried to catch Tuna's eyes, but they were rage and spit and hunger. Screaming and beating the bars with his fists. His arms were bruised and pocked with puncture wounds, and still he flailed.

Punctures?

Wyatt caught Tuna's wrist for a half second. The wounds were fresh. He let go and rounded on the nurse. "You're experimenting on him?"

"There was some serum left." The nurse didn't flinch. "I'm using the protocols the Council set up."

"Forget the protocols!" Wyatt yelled. "That's my friend!"

"Everybody back here," the nurse said, "is somebody's friend. What makes yours special?"

"I . . . " Wyatt hesitated. "That's not what I meant."

"Leave the caboose to me, Conductor." The nurse pushed Wyatt toward the door. "You know the rules. Nobody matters more than the train."

Wyatt pulled the red door open, then whispered, "And everybody ends up in the caboose."

RYLE

As soon as Wyatt left the map car, Ryle had traced the circular train loop with a finger, memorizing the route. She continued until she reached the westernmost turn at Salt Lake. *If we can just make Utah,* she told herself.

She tapped a finger on the outskirts of Fort Collins. "That's where we'll meet you, Parcheesi," she whispered. But why steal the train if she could maybe trick Wyatt into turning the train over to her?

Above Ryle, the hatch door slid open, and heavy boots hit the floor. It wasn't Wyatt. His step was light and quick, like a coyote. This person was a thunder-footed St. Bernard.

Diesel.

She could smell him, a sour tang of sweat mixed with Axe body spray. *Play it cool,* she told herself and rolled the map up. "Wyatt isn't here, Diesel."

"I always know where Wyatt is," Diesel said. "I've got eyes and ears all over this train."

"Sounds messy."

"What does?"

"Having eyes and ears all over the train." She smirked. "Bet it stinks as bad as a zombie. Worse, probably."

"You think you're funny?" Diesel said. "I don't like girls

who think they're funny and take a job that's rightfully mine."

Here it comes, Ryle thought.

Diesel grabbed her shoulder. His hand was huge, and he was strong enough to spin her easily.

She snapped her bō out. "Back off."

"Whoa," Diesel said. "You got spunk." A grinch-like grin split his face. "I like spunk."

It wasn't the reaction she was expecting. It threw her for a second, and she relaxed long enough for Diesel to grab her wrist. The bō slipped from her fingers and clattered on the floorboards.

Diesel shoved her into a seat and scooped up the bō. He tested its weight in his hands, tossing it back and forth. "I like this, too," he said. "Think I'll keep it."

Ryle shrugged, pretending not to care, although she wanted to punch him. Her mom had two golden retrievers. They took turns stealing each other's chew toys. They played the game till one got bored of the toys. Kids like Diesel weren't much more complicated than goldens.

"You don't care?" Diesel said.

She shrugged again. "It's just a stick."

It wasn't true, of course. The bō belonged to her grandmother, who had used it to knock apples from the trees in their backyard. When Ryle had fled home, it was the first thing she grabbed, and it had saved her life more times than she could count. She knew that if she demanded it, Diesel would keep it. Like a dog with a stolen toy.

Above them, the hatch flew open, and Festus dropped through. "Wyatt's on his way back. It went fast, Big D."

"What went fast?" Ryle couldn't help it. Curiosity always got the better of her.

"That's our business," Diesel said. "Which means it's none of yours."

"Yeah, none yer business," Festus repeated.

"How many times were you dropped on your head as a baby?" Ryle asked.

Festus counted on his fingers. "Three?"

"Oh, no. I'm sorry." She couldn't believe this kid. "I was joking."

"That's a good one." Festus laughed. "I like jokes. It means we're friends."

"Stop laughing and take this." Diesel shoved the bō into Festus' hands. "Lock it up in my treasure chest."

"Don't it belong to her?" Festus said.

"It did." He winked at Ryle. "Now it belongs to me."

"If you say so, but that don't seem right," Festus said, then exited the map car through the hatch, the staff swinging behind him like a pendulum.

"Before your attitude changed my mind, I was gonna clue you in on a surprise for Wyatt." Diesel winked at Ryle. "You like surprises, right?"

"Oh, I love surprises." She ran her fingers through her hair. Rage bubbled inside her. She wanted to force him to give the bō back. To teach him a lesson. But that might ruin Parcheesi's plan, and she had come too far to throw it all away. "More than your tiny brain can imagine."

15

DIESEL

The high moon was waxing and the sky mostly clear when Diesel opened three padlocks and removed the chains securing the ATVs to the flatcar. He chose the newer ATV for its bigger engine and softer seat. He stored arrows under the cushion and strapped the hunting bow he'd "borrowed" from the armory across his back.

"Gimme a push," he told Festus, who was yawning from being awakened at two a.m.

Festus huffed an icy breath and pushed the ATV to the ramp. "You gonna use the lift?"

"Unless this thing can fly."

"It don't, does it?"

Diesel waved his flashlight in Festus' eyes. "No, stupid, it rolls."

They guided the ATV onto the ramp and used the hydraulics to lower the ramp until it almost touched the ground. The landscape was rolling by, and the buildings were getting sparser. Despite the cold, sweat rolled down Diesel's back.

"I'm going to start the ATV," Diesel explained slowly. "Wait for my signal—"

Festus stuffed both hands into his armpits. "What signal?"

"Two thumbs-up. Like this." He demonstrated. "Then push the red handle till the ramp drops. It's going to be loud, so don't freak out."

"Gotcha, Big D." Festus looked at the control board, eyes darting. "When do I raise up the ramp?"

"After I drive the ATVs off, duh."

"I wait for your signal again?"

Diesel closed his eyes and sighed. "I've explained it a hundred times. Raise the ramp. Push the green handle to the left. Swing the ramp back onto the flatcar. Lock it with the safety chain. Got it?"

"Red up, then back. Green to the left."

"Right."

"Green to the right?"

"No, left."

"You said left, right?"

"Bruh! Green to the left!"

"Left?"

"Correct!"

Festus wiped his nose with a sleeve. "Don't be mad, Big D. I'm doing my best to be a good friend."

"Then use those floppy ears for something besides decoration." Diesel started the ATV and gave the signal. "Thumbs-up, Festus!"

Festus' face fell, but he pulled the red handle back and the ramp rose.

"Push!" Diesel yelled. "Not pull!"

Festus panicked and pushed the handle forward. The ramp lowered. Diesel rolled onto the ground and veered away from the train. When he looked over his shoulder, the ramp was swinging back into place.

Miracles did happen. Festus had done something right. "Time to rustle up some zombies," Diesel said and headed across the dark, deep plains.

16

RYLE

At six the next morning, the zombie train rolled through light snow falling on Loveland at five mph. Though it had to be below freezing, Ryle propped her feet on the locomotive's rear railing, feeling human after a good sleep. In the night, they had quietly passed the Ish Reservoir and Campion, and the longer she rode the train, the more at home she felt. The sun had risen behind her, and a flock of geese floated by. She sighed contentedly in the down coat Tater had lent her. Was it a mistake to stick to Parcheesi's plan?

At the other end of the train, the riders had gathered for Marti's burial. Which is why she and Vash were hanging out on the locomotive. It felt weird to intrude. It also gave Vash the chance to buddy up to Pez.

"But that makes no sense!" Vash yelled.

Ryle jumped to her feet and ran to the cab. She threw the door open and rushed past the hot engines to the control board. Pez was using a large crescent wrench to ward off Vash, who was screaming and throwing hands.

"Lucille's locomotive is ninety-eight-and-a-half feet long," Pez bellowed. "And near fifteen feet tall. She weighs 270 tons, and her prime mover's two sixteen-cylinder diesel engines with turbochargers, which we don't use no turbos 'cause they put too much stress on the valves! Which is why the second engine's on its last leg!"

Vash pointed to a large white tank. "What's that, then?"

"I told you!" Pez yelled back. "It's fuel for emergencies!"

Ryle whistled. "Time out!"

Vash didn't even look her way. "Raising the speed five miles an hour will only use five percent more fuel, and we won't get attacked."

"One, Lucille's needing maintenance soon. She's done lost her second engine." Pez looked between Ryle and Vash. "Two, Cheddar said we don't need no more speed to outrun zombies."

"Zombies aren't the only things out there, dummy," Vash said.

Pez cut his eyes at her. "What *things* are you talking about?"

"Vash! Think!" Ryle put an arm around Vash and pulled her close. It might look like a sisterly hug, but it was a signal for Vash to shut it. "Hey, Pez?" Ryle's voice brightened. "Where did you learn how to be a driver?"

"Driver?" Pez said. "You don't drive a train. It ain't no car."

"He's an engineer," Vash said quickly. "Come on, girl. Everybody knows that."

Nice save. That got him. Ryle smiled at Pez. "My bad. Engineer."

"My grandpa was the one who taught me," Pez said, looking bashful.

Vash cleared her throat. "Dude, she's buttering you—ow! Stop pinching me!"

"Shh!" Ryle forced a smile. "Pez is telling us a story about his grandpa. Was he an engineer, too?"

"He worked for Union Pacific," Pez said, still oblivious. "After he took a pension, he worked in Cheyenne at the railroad museum, telling tourists all about trains."

Vash nodded along. "That's real nice."

"You making fun of my grandpa?" Pez said.

"She wasn't making fun," Ryle said quickly. "Right, Vash?"

"Cut me some slack," Vash whispered. "I say something nice and look what happens."

"Try not being a smart aleck," Ryle whispered back. "So, Pez, this was your grandpa's engine?"

"Locomotive," he said.

"Locomotive. Right. How did the riders find it?"

"I was hiding in the rail yard when Wyatt and his brother showed up. They wanted a train to outrun the zombies." He puffed up, all proud. "And they wanted me to engineer."

"Annnnd the rest is history." Vash pretended to suppress a yawn. "Fascinating story."

Ryle smiled. "Thanks for your story, Pez. Did you say Wyatt has a brother?"

"He did." Pez looked down. "Reckon he still does."

"Vash, let's take a walk," she said.

Vash begrudgingly followed Ryle from the cab. "What? I'm in trouble now?"

"Why did you disrespect that kid by yawning at him?" Ryle turned and hissed freezing breath at Vash. "Parcheesi's plan was to learn to run a locomotive, not make the engineer want to kill you."

"D'you think they'll figure it out?" Vash asked, shivering. "Wyatt don't look like a dummy, and that Cheddar knows more algebra than a math teacher."

"Yeah, they smart," Ryle said. "We better keep our lips pinched tight."

"But your plan—"

"Parcheesi's plan. And where's the coat Tater lent you?"

"It's too hot in the cab for that coat." Vash folded her arms to keep warm. "They ain't gonna like us hijacking their train. And Pez ain't so bad once you get to know him."

"Why did you argue with him, if he's not so bad?"

"I only fight with folks I like." Then Vash smiled slyly. "You know, these are good people. They could be family. We don't have to go through with it."

"It?"

"*It.*"

Ryle put a finger to her lips. "We've been watching this train for weeks. We're not the only ones, so we're doing them a favor. Although . . ."

"Although what?" Vash said. "What no good are you up to?"

"You'll see. Now get back in there and learn how to drive Lucille—"

"Engineer."

"—while I go to liberate my bō. Maybe even visit the caboose."

"But it's off-limits."

Ryle grinned. She loved forbidden places. It made them much more fun to visit.

17

WYATT

When you lived on a train that never stopped, prairie burials were a necessity. That fact didn't make them any easier for Wyatt, whose first act as conductor had been putting the original conductor out of her misery and whose second job was sending the most recent conductor to the afterlife.

The prairie burials had started after Ricky turned, and they had left him on the tracks. He'd run after the train until he was exhausted. He called out, "Please don't leave me out here alone," then fell to the ground, crying. It was so gut-wrenching, they made a new rule. Nobody would be dumped on the tracks again.

"Thanks for coming this morning," he told the older riders gathered on the helipad at daybreak to pay their respects. The littles were still under lockdown, and everyone attending was shivering in their coats and constantly looking over their shoulders. Who could blame them? Wyatt felt the exact same way. Only he had to hide it. "Marti liked things simple, so that's how we're going to keep it."

Wyatt looked down at Marti's body and bowed his head. "Marti conducted the train for three-and-a-half circles, and she gave the train what was left of her life."

"She gave what was left of her life," the riders chanted in response, their words forming white clouds above their heads.

Lucille had given eleven kids back to the earth. Eleven, Wyatt thought as he stared at Marti's body now bundled in burlap flour bags. She had been twelve years and eight months old. Only a few months older than Wyatt. There would be no history or record books to remember her by, but Lucille would. The little ones would. Wyatt would also, in the time he had left before it was flour bags for him, too.

"Turn away, please," Wyatt said.

When all their backs were turned, he raised his hand, then dropped it. Cheddar quietly rolled Marti's body over the side. It tumbled into the tall prairie grass that ran alongside the track and disappeared. Then Wyatt heard a sob. He looked back and saw Cheddar comforting Ginny. In school Ched had been bully bait. Now he was the best human alive.

One by one the riders drifted away from the helipad, until Wyatt was left alone.

"Wyatt?" Ryle called him with a wave. Her expression made her look frightened and excited at the same time.

He thought she was in the cab with Pez. Why was she on the helipad?

Silently she pointed northeast to a wide horizon of farmland turned prairie. A shadow stretched across it, maybe a mile wide and a half mile deep. The shadow was moving and looked like a massive herd of animals.

"Are those buffalo?" she said.

"We should be so lucky," Wyatt said and tugged at the yellow band on his wrist. "It's the eastern zombie herd, the one we avoid at all costs." As far as the eye could see, all zombies. "It doesn't usually stray this far west. I'll send our best outriders, Beanie and Kiki, to check it out." He put a finger to his lips. "Let's keep this quiet."

"You're not going to tell the Council?"

"It might be nothing. No reason to freak everybody out. They're still feeling jittery over Marti."

"You're the conductor." She shook her head then looked around, alarmed. "Is the train slowing down?"

She was right. Lucille was just inching forward. "What now?" he said and headed for the locomotive. "You coming with, brakeman?"

"Later," she said. "I've got business to take care of."

18

WYATT

By the time Wyatt reached the engineer's cab, Pez was screaming and Vash had Festus pinned against the control board.

"Never touch the gauges!" Pez bellowed. "Nobody touches the gauges but the engineers!"

Vash gave Festus a hard shake. "Yeah! Nobody but the engineers!"

"Whoa! Guys!" Wyatt pulled them apart. "Calm down! Vash, let loose of Festus' hair."

Vash reluctantly released him. "Little rat tried to stop Lucille!"

"Not stop," Festus protested. "Slow her down for Diesel."

"Pez, Vash, get us back up to speed." Wyatt hauled Festus past the engines and cooling fans to the rear door. "That stunt earned you three days latrine duty. Where's Diesel?"

"He's . . . he's . . . "

"He's what?"

"I was out hunting." Diesel entered the cab, a small, field-dressed buck slung over his shoulders. "You didn't hear me take the ATV? Oh, that's right. You're too busy 'conducting.'"

Wyatt motioned for Diesel to follow him back out to the deck. "You made Festus slow down the train? So you could go hunting?"

"No, bruh! It was so I could reload the ATV." Diesel dropped the deer carcass onto the platform. "Parking on a moving flatcar's a nightmare."

"There are two deep freezers full of meat," Wyatt said. "We don't need more, and we don't need blood all over the locomotive deck."

"Bruh! My bad." Diesel punched Wyatt's shoulder. "Do me a solid and tell Tater to finish dressing this thing. I'll take my steak rare."

Diesel stepped over the deer. Festus jumped over it and followed. They high fived and laughed.

Ryle was right. They were boneheads. Wyatt sighed and rolled the carcass over the side of the locomotive and on to the embankment, but it wasn't enough. A dead deer meant blood. Zombie fresh had noses like bottle flies, so they could smell blood miles away. Wyatt knew he had to get the deer away from the tracks. He jumped down, landing in gravel.

"I'm sorry," he said and hauled it a hundred yards into mist-covered prairie.

Killing the deer was a waste of life. That's what Diesel was. A waster, not a maker. Wyatt looked out across the grasslands. It was colder than a slushie, and the plains were eerily quiet, except for a faint clicking noise. His gut said he wasn't alone. He waited and watched. Were his ears just playing tricks? He was about to give up and run back to the train when a zombie fresh appeared from the mist.

It looked like it had raided a 1980s gym locker. It was unnaturally tall with poofed-up frizzy hair held up by a rainbow headband. It wore tiny lime-green gym shorts and matching tube socks with low-top white Nikes. The zombie looked confused, then it took a deep breath, like it was smelling blood in the air, and turned toward the carcass.

"Nice zombie," Wyatt said soothingly. "You don't want to eat me, right?" He took a step away from the deer. His boot slipped on the snowy grass, and in a heartbeat, he knew there was no way to outrun this thing. He slowly drew his paintball gun. "Let's make a deal. You take the meat, and I'll mosey on."

The zombie pounced on the deer, its jaws clacking and drool running down the side of its mouth. For a second Wyatt thought it had understood and dived right in, but then it stood up and set its bloodshot eyes on him.

"Son of a biscuit," he whispered.

The zombie fresh charged, frizzy hair bobbing wildly. Wyatt aimed, and with a quick pull of the trigger—*thwip!*—a purple paintball burst hit the zombie between the eyes. The zombie shook its head, paint obliterating its vision.

"Bet you didn't see that coming," Wyatt said.

The bewildered zombie swayed, then face-planted, smearing purple paint on the frozen grass. Undeterred, it kept crawling for Wyatt, clicking and wailing. Wyatt holstered the paintball gun and stepped away, thinking that it was a weird place for a zombie fresh to be.

Wyatt surveyed the lay of the land. The mountains filled the western sky. Peaks half covered with snow. Their days of clear, easy running were ending. Winter would be here soon. But for now, fields of tall grasses blowing in the wind stretched to the horizon. Not a human in sight. So why did his skin crawl, like somebody was watching his every move?

19

DIESEL

"Wyatt's such a moron," Diesel told Festus five minutes later. "I give him fresh meat, and he throws it back like a spit-licked Big Mac."

"Wish I had me a Big Mac," Festus said.

They stood atop the second boxcar, teeth chattering in the icy wind, watching Wyatt climbing onto the locomotive after shooting the zombie fresh.

"Can you believe that?" Diesel said. "Wyatt almost gets himself eaten over one dead deer, and he doesn't even know about the other four I killed."

Festus whistled. "Four! That many so fast?"

"It was too easy."

"Think your plan will work?"

"It's a perfect plan. Zombies find food, they stick close by," Diesel said. "It's all instinct. Next time we roll through, this field will be dirty with them."

"But zombies won't stop Lucille."

"I'm not trying to stop the train, stupid," Diesel said, tapping his temple. "I'm trying to stop Wyatt. The train gets attacked, and he chokes. Totally messes up. He's a loser. I save everybody and take over as conductor."

"I'll be the conductor's best friend."

"Yeah, sure." Diesel opened the boxcar hatch. "Time to do your five-finger discount thing."

Festus shinnied through the opening. Diesel watched him check behind the shelving, then give the thumbs-up. Diesel dropped down into the boxcar.

He took two sacks from a hook on the wall in the corner. He shoved one into Festus' hands. "Fill it up with those canned apples. I'm sick of beans and rice."

"Won't they know we took it?"

"If anybody asks, we'll blame the strandeds," Diesel said. "They get purged, and Wyatt walks the plank. Perfect plan."

"Yeah, perfect."

They quickly cherry-picked the shelves for the best stuff, and when they were finished, the bags were almost too heavy to lift.

"Meet you in my sleeper compartment," Diesel said as Festus shinnied back onto the roof and hoisted up the bags. "Hide the cans in my footlocker."

Festus saluted. "You got it, Big D."

Diesel followed, then stopped short. "What was that?" He quickly scanned the shelves and the corners of the car. Nothing there. His ears must be playing tricks. With a shrug, he mumbled, "Like taking candy from a baby."

RYLE

The second boxcar was still. Dust motes floated down, lit by the bright sunlight seeping through the hatch. It was dark inside the car, and it smelled of creosote and oil. In the corner, a cabinet door opened, and Ryle unfolded herself. She knocked dust from her clothes, then pulled cobwebs from her hair.

She scanned the shelves. The apples and Vienna sausages were gone.

"Blame us for your thieving?" she said. "Let's see what happens when the baby steals her candy back."

The train was nearing Fort Collins when Ryle slipped silently into the sleeping car. The compartment doors were covered with posters and hand-drawn artwork. Except the last door, which was labeled: PRIVATE KEEP OUT.

Diesel.

She popped the lock with a fork and slipped inside. The air stank of vinegar and garlic, but it was a surprisingly neat space. Bed made. Clothes hung up. Diesel had also collected comforts. A box fan, a stack of manga, and a Nintendo Switch.

Her bō was resting against the wall. She grabbed it.

At the foot of the bed, Ryle spotted an army footlocker. It was padlocked, but she used the fork to pick it. The locker contained more surprises. A box of Snickers. Body armor. Helmet. Ammo belt. Ammo. *Hmm*. Guns were banned from the train.

Wyatt should know about this. She put the stuff back and was about to lock up when the compartment door eased open.

She flattened herself against the wall. If this were the wilderness, she'd throw a punch to the face, then escape. But when you plan to hijack a train, beating up your host is not a viable strategy.

The door slid open a bit more, and Ryle held her breath. Tater ducked into the compartment.

Tater?

He was dressed in jeans and a T-shirt, sneakers in hand. He crept to Diesel's stack of manga. He slid a couple of issues out as Ryle snuck up behind him.

"Hi, Tater," she whispered. "Who's watching the tots?"

Tater squeaked, and Ryle clapped a hand over his mouth.

"It's okay," she whispered. "Why are you here?"

"This was my sister's room," Tater said, after he'd pried her hand from his mouth. "But Diesel claimed all her stuff, after . . . Please don't tell on me."

He suddenly didn't seem so grouchy. "What was your sister's name?" Ryle asked.

"Kendra."

"Where's Kendra now?"

The manga fell to the floor. Ryle had a good idea what that meant. His sister had turned, and he wanted something to remember her by.

Ginny's sharp whisper came from outside the compartment. "Tater? Where'd you go?"

So he had a lookout. Smart. Ryle picked up the comics and gave them to Tater. "This'll be our secret," she said.

Tater shot from the room like a spooked jackrabbit. He dropped a sneaker, then hastily grabbed it, leaving the door swinging.

Ryle exhaled. Be more careful next time. You know better than to forget the escape route. There always has to be a way out.

She slipped into the corridor, then locked the door behind her. She followed the aisle to the next car, walked into the crowded dining car like she owned it, and spotted Vash, Cheddar, and Wyatt having a discussion with Diesel, right before the train horn blew three long blasts.

"Battle stations!" Wyatt yelled and the kids scattered. "Riders, move out! Vash, Ryle, you're with me."

Vash pumped a fist. "Battle stations! Yes!"

"Ched," Wyatt said. "Stick to the drills as practiced. Don't fire without orders." He turned back to Diesel. "Got that?"

"Yes, *Conductor*," Diesel said, then shoved past Ryle, barking orders to Festus and a posse of boys who followed him like pied piper rats.

"Three blasts on the horn?" Ryle asked when she caught up with Wyatt. "What's that mean?"

"A warning from Pez," he said. "Cleanup on aisle five."

"Clean up on what-what?"

"Something's blocking the rails," he said. "Something big."

21

WYATT

"Cleanup on aisle five," Wyatt announced over the PA from the locomotive cab. "This is not a drill." He hung up the mic and turned to Pez and Vash. "You two keep Lucille steady. Ryle, stay put."

"Yes sir," they said in tandem.

Wyatt swung down from the rear ladder to the ground, and Ryle jumped down after him. The tracks ran alongside a crumbling rural highway next to the old Colina Mariposa Natural Area. Ponderosa pine saplings dotted the sunbaked landscape like irregular teeth in a saw blade, their morning shadows stretching out. Blue grama grass and sagebrush rustled in the harsh wind, and the saplings waved back and forth like they were warning the train away.

"Thought I told you to wait," Wyatt said.

"One, I don't take orders," she said. "Two, why miss all the fun?"

"A feral mob is trying to stop the train. This is your idea of fun?"

"Are ferals mean and nasty and armed to the teeth?"

"Ninety percent of the time."

"Then yeah, that's my idea of fun."

They both laughed and took off running, barely ahead

of the train. Lucille's brakes hissed as she slowed but slowing wasn't stopping. In the distance, the snow-dusted ruins of Fort Collins rose from the prairie.

Wyatt slowed to a trot and pointed ahead. He could make out faces now, and his throat tightened with pity. Small kids, mostly. Unarmed except for a few long sticks.

"Do you do this often?" she said as she pulled up beside him. "Clearing ferals off the tracks? You don't run them down?"

"Run them down?" he said, taken aback. "They're people, just like us. What kind of monster do you think I am?"

"I'm sorry. I didn't mean . . . Listen," she said and grabbed his shoulder. "These are strandeds, not ferals, and there's something I need to tell you before—"

Wh-hisk!

An arrow shot past Wyatt's head and disappeared into the pack of strandeds. One of them screamed and the whole pack dropped to the ground.

"Who fired that?" Wyatt said, looking around.

Ryle pointed back at the locomotive. "Diesel did!"

Diesel stood atop Lucille, compound bow in hand.

"Stand down!" Wyatt yelled. He turned and ran back toward the train. There was steam in his lungs and fire in his chest, and black bees swarmed his vision. Diesel nocked another arrow. Wyatt would never get there in time. "Stop!" he yelled.

Diesel fired again just as Vash scrambled out of the cabin window and grabbed his leg. The shot whistled harmlessly through the grass.

"That was my last hunting arrow!" Diesel yelled.

"Be glad it's not your last tooth!" Vash yelled back, yanking his pants leg.

The air horn sounded, and Pez's voice came over the PA. "Boss! Lucille can't stop in time!"

"Try it anyway!" Wyatt yelled through ragged breaths. "Vash! Forget about Diesel and grab the first-aid kit!"

Brakes hit the locomotive's wheels and a high-pitched squeal filled the air.

Lucille rolled on.

A moment later Vash jumped down from the locomotive and ran toward Wyatt. He held out a hand for the kit, but she raced past him. When she reached the strandeds, the kids' circle opened to welcome her. There were at least a dozen kids, mostly little ones barely as tall as her waist, shaking violently from the cold. Their clothes and hair were dirty and ragged. Their cheeks were scarred with almost-healed wounds in the shape of a chain link. Someone had branded them!

"Ryle, what's going on?" Wyatt asked when they reached the group.

He knew he was taking a big chance getting so close. The kids looked pathetic. No source of food or water for a dozen miles. Why were they here? What did they want? Why hadn't they scattered when Diesel fired? Where were their freaking coats?

Ryle ignored him. Vash pawed through the first-aid kit. Tore open two bandage packets and a tube of antibiotic cream. But the wounded girl pushed her aside and struggled to stand.

"Parch," Ryle said. "Sit down."

But the girl got to her feet. She was a few inches shorter than Ryle. Black rings under her gray eyes. Her mousy hair a mud dauber's nest covering her face. The arrow had struck her thigh, and blood seeped through her jeans.

Then she pushed her hair aside, and Wyatt recognized the zigzagged nose that Marti had broken in a fight.

"Hey, little brother," the girl said. "Miss me?"

"Parcheesi?" Wyatt shook his head. "We thought you were dead."

"Not surprised," she said. "Since that's how you losers left me."

22

WYATT

The engine crawled across the flat landscape, steel wheels creaking on the steel rails. A thin layer of snow swirled around the tracks as the stranded children stared at the train, their faces hidden by dirt and hunger, their clothes too thin for the bitter cold.

"Don't stand there gawking, kids," Parcheesi said. "Get on the freaking train." When none of them moved, she tried to get to her feet to make them.

"Sit down before you pass out," Wyatt said. "We'll bring a stretcher."

"You shot me," Parcheesi said. "So bite me."

"That bonehead Diesel shot you," Vash said. She tried to grab the arrow sticking out of Parcheesi's leg, but Parcheesi smacked her.

Ryle pulled the little ones into a hug like a mama duck gathering her brood. "You guys okay?" she asked. "Sorry we scared you like that."

"Back up a minute," Wyatt said, anger flaring. He had vouched for her. "You know them?"

"We split up a couple weeks ago," Ryle said. "Parcheesi took most of the crew, and I took the rest."

"That doesn't make any sense," he said. Maybe it did.

He caught her eye and shook his head, a silent accusation. "You're lucky we didn't run over you, Parcheesi. Didn't you see the train?"

"See it?" Parcheesi said and laughed. "Little brother, we were waiting for it." She stretched out her wounded leg. Blood had soaked her jeans.

"Let's get you to Cheddar," Wyatt said.

"Don't need Cheeseboy's help," Parcheesi said. "Just rub a little spit on it."

A little kid hocked a loogie.

Vash put up a hand to stop him. "Don't spit on a wound, bonehead."

Wyatt was caught in a rapidly moving stream of emotions—doubts and fear washed over him. He pulled Ryle aside and whispered, "When you got on the train, I said we don't keep secrets."

"Tell Diesel that," Ryle said.

She threw Parcheesi's arm over her shoulder. Together, Ryle, Vash, and Parcheesi stumbled toward the train. The little ones formed two lines, tallest to shortest, and followed them like obedient soldiers.

Wyatt waved his arms to signal Pez. A single horn blast answered him. If they didn't get on, they'd get left. "Too slow!" he barked at Ryle. He grabbed Parcheesi by the belt and lifted her over his shoulder. "You're losing blood fast."

"You got strong," Parcheesi said, sounding woozy.

"Don't think you're getting away with this," he said. "Ryle, you owe me an explanation. You owe us all one."

"You going to let a little punk talk to you like that, Ry-Ry?" Parcheesi slurred.

Ryle ran a hand through her hair. "When Parcheesi's patched up," she said, "we can have a sit down."

"Parcheesi's the reason we started the vouching!" Wyatt couldn't bite back his anger any longer. "Why's she trying to get back on the train?"

"Because we found the zombie cure," Parcheesi mumbled. "Nirvana."

23

RYLE

By midmorning the train was rolling through Fort Collins, and Ryle sat next to Parcheesi on a bed in the warm infirmary car. Snow was falling outside, and once again Ryle thanked heaven for electric heaters. Cheddar had cleaned and bandaged Parcheesi's wound and given her meds. When Parch woke up, they'd hijack the train like they'd planned. So why did Ryle feel so guilty?

Parcheesi was tough. But being a leader was more than being tough. Parcheesi's littles were dirty. They had bad cuts and bruises. Those horrible brands on their cheeks.

They'd all devoured Tater's oatmeal like locusts. Then they were given clean clothes and marched to the showers, and they didn't even whine when sent to bed after breakfast. After they were asleep, Ryle had returned to the infirmary to find maps scattered on Parcheesi's bunk. Parcheesi, practically dead to the world, clutched one. The route from Denver to Seattle was highlighted in green.

"Way to make it obvious, *boss*," Ryle had said, folding up the map.

From then until noon, Parcheesi talked under her breath. The arrow had pierced her thigh muscle. Cheddar thought the wound would heal clean, yet sweat soaked her hair. Her breath sounded ragged, and she licked her chapped lips over and over again.

"Parch—"

Parcheesi's eyes popped open. She grabbed Ryle's thumb and fingers and growled, "It's all lies."

"What is?"

"Nirvana. Only used it to get your . . . help."

Ryle pulled against Parcheesi's iron grip. When did Parcheesi get so stupid strong? Was she delirious? Or was she telling the truth?

"She's watching . . . rounding up big herds . . . "

Parcheesi's eyes rolled back, and her head fell onto the pillow.

What? Ryle rubbed the sore thumb. Had something happened since they'd split up? Nirvana was all lies? No. That couldn't be right.

She tucked the blanket under Parcheesi's chin. Parch rolled onto her side and sighed. Sleep found her, and an hour later when Wyatt entered the infirmary, she hadn't stirred.

"Ryle." Wyatt stood at the door, arms crossed. "It's time for the truth."

24

RYLE

"I keep asking questions," Wyatt said a few minutes later, "and you keep answering with fairy tales."

They were sitting on the helipad. The bitter wind had turned their faces sore, and the sky was packed with darkening clouds. Beyond them, the plains of northern Colorado spread out like a grass-covered table.

"Nirvana is . . . " If you say it, Ryle thought, there's no going back. "Not a fairy tale."

Wyatt shook his head. "Nirvana's a lie."

"You're calling me a liar?"

"Not a liar," he said. "Maybe Parcheesi filled your head with stories. She tried the same thing on us."

"Shut up," Ryle said. "Don't treat me like some stupid little girl."

"I don't mean—"

"Doesn't matter what you mean," she said. "It matters what you do."

"Speak your mind." Wyatt turned up the collar of his down coat. "Then I'll tell you what we'll do."

Ryle flexed her jaw like she was chewing on his words, mashing them into paste. "Nirvana's a naval facility off the coast near Seattle. It's where the government people were evacuated."

Wyatt looked up at the flurries dropping from the overcast sky. "Oh, it's a naval facility now. Parcheesi's added new details to her lies."

"Let me finish." Ryle sighed. "After Denver burned, Vash and I hid out with a couple of ex-marines from Vash's neighborhood. After a few days of protecting us from zombies, they told us about Nirvana and asked if we wanted to go."

"And you said yes? It was desperate times, but c'mon."

Ryle shrugged. "We found a car and took I-70 west. It went great till we hit barricades at the Utah border. We saw these handmade signs saying *Welcome to Paradise*. But the army wasn't letting anybody through, and then, the marines turned."

He cocked an eyebrow. "So you got kicked out of paradise?"

"Only from Utah," she said. "But listen, Parcheesi says that Nirvana's a real research facility. Scientists were working on a cure before any of this started."

"You want Lucille to take you there?"

"A cure, Wy. A chance that some of us might live. Hope."

Wyatt shook his head. "False hope is worse than no hope."

"Didn't you say that any hope is worth it? Look, I checked your maps. If we can make Utah, then we can make Salt Lake. From there, it's a straight shot to Seattle, and we're home free."

"Not that simple." Wyatt shook his head. "Not that easy."

"It can be," she said, looking out at the horizon and rubbing her sore thumb.

"Once we leave the safety of the loop—what then?"

"You don't have a choice."

"Is that a threat?" Wyatt asked. "Because I vouched for you, and you paid me back by betraying my trust."

"It's not a threat," she said softly, "it's reality. Riding the loop can't stop time, and time's going to kill us all."

25

WYATT

An hour later the train was ten miles northeast of Fort Collins and crawling across the plains. Every kid over ten was packed into the observatory car, and Wyatt's hands were shaking, and not from the cold. Some people had nerves of steel talking to groups. His were pudding.

"Everybody here?" he asked. He'd spent the time since Ryle's confession talking to the Council, and they'd all reluctantly listened about Nirvana. Now he had to share the same info with all the riders.

"Council is present," Cheddar said, pointing to himself and Tater.

"That's all of my crew," Ryle said.

"Diesel's posse in the house," Diesel said.

"House? But this is a train," Festus said, earning him a head smack. "Ow! But it is, Big D."

"No more this crew or that posse," Wyatt said. "I'm the conductor, and I say that we're all riders now." Wyatt glanced around the observatory car. "If y'all haven't heard, there's a girl in the infirmary because somebody didn't follow orders."

All eyes turned to Diesel. "Whatever, bruh," he said and pretended to dust off his Tony Lama boots. "I acted on the intel at hand."

"Your intelligence has earned you two weeks' latrine duty."

Once a day all riders took a turn emptying the toilet tanks. It was the worst duty on the train, and nobody had ever pulled more than five days straight. Two weeks? It was a life sentence.

"Like I said." Diesel sucked his teeth. "Whatever."

Wyatt ignored him. The riders needed a calm leader, not an argument. "Council rules say all train business gets discussed, and riders get a vote in big decisions," he said. "Here's the deal. Ryle knows a place. A military base. Code name Nirvana—"

The car erupted with excited voices.

Ginny, Tater's assistant, stood up. "Nirvana's a forbidden word."

It'd been Marti's decision to ban the word, and Wyatt was through with policies Marti had made from fear. He whistled. "Keep interrupting, and I'll make this decision by myself."

"Shut it, losers!" Diesel said. "Let's hear our fearless leader out."

Wyatt pointed at Diesel to silence him then said, "Ryle? You're up."

"Nirvana"—Ryle cleared her throat—"is more than a military base."

She retold the story in simple words. Broke it down for

the younger kids so they'd understand. When she finished, their excited chatter grew louder.

Wyatt silenced them again. "There might be a Nirvana, but there also might be nothing there. Worse than nothing. We've got enough food, water, and fuel to last for years if we play our cards right. We're safe on the loop."

"Except for the parasite," Cheddar said.

"We checked the map," Wyatt said. "It shows a spur from Salt Lake to Seattle, but we don't know if there's even a track anymore."

"You so suck as a salesman," Vash said.

Ryle clapped a hand over Vash's mouth. "Shut it."

"But maybe hope matters more than certainty," Wyatt said. "So we can either survive short term." He lifted his hands to mimic a scale. "Or take a chance at living."

"You're only saying that," Diesel said, "because you're next to turn."

"Maybe I am," Wyatt said. "But it's my job as conductor to do what's best for everyone." He cut Diesel an acid look. "Even you."

"What're you saying?" Diesel said. "We either follow you or get purged?"

"That's not—" Wyatt began.

"Without a cure," Ryle said, "you either get eaten by zombie fresh or become zombie fresh. That's the cold, hard reality."

Diesel laughed. He checked to see if his posse was going along. No laughter. Only whispers of curiosity and fear. "For older kids like us, living a few more months sounds sweet," he said. "What've we got to lose, right? One day"—he snapped his fingers—"something clicks, and we're not hungry for Snickers. Now we want brains, and we turn as wild as a pack of wolves."

"Not wolves," Cheddar said. "Zombie fresh are hosts of progressively destructive parasites, and wolves are alpha predators essential to an ecosystem. They don't eat brains."

"Whatever, Cheeseboy," Diesel continued. "What about the little brats? What've they got to lose by leaving the loop?"

All eyes turned to Wyatt.

He could see the fear, hope, and yearning in their faces. When he swallowed, there was gravel in his throat. "We keep Lucille running," he said. "That hasn't changed."

Ginny raised her hand. "The last two times hunting parties went out, they ran into ferals. What if there are more of them outside the loop?"

"I'm sick of what-ifs," Diesel said. "You babies are all soft."

"Thank you for the bitter, angry voice in this discussion," Wyatt said. "Anybody got more questions?"

Ginny raised her hand again. "How long's it take to get to Seattle?"

"Five months to be semi-exact," Cheddar said, cleaning his glasses with his shirttail. "However, routes west travel through the Rockies, and there's a snowpack to contend with. If the train gets stranded, a modern Donner Party is a real possibility. So the trip must begin—" He put his glasses back on. "Immediately."

"Train's going the wrong way to start immediately," Wyatt said.

"We could execute a turnaround," Cheddar said. "By using the switchback in Cheyenne. Then we retrace the western route back into the Rockies. The almanac predicts a few days of mild weather before the snows begin to fall, and in Cheyenne we could resupply."

"Sounds like you got all it planned out," Wyatt said. "How long have you been thinking about this?"

"About Nirvana?" Cheddar grinned. "Approximately an hour, but an emergency turnaround? Infinitely longer."

"Time for a vote," Wyatt said. "Everybody put your heads down and close your eyes. Those in favor of running the loop," he said, "raise your hands."

Half the riders raised their hands. Festus was among them. Diesel's hands stayed in his pockets.

"Got it," Wyatt said. "Now those for Nirvana, raise your hands."

The rest of the hands lifted. Diesel raised a clenched fist.

"Hands down," Wyatt said. "Eyes open."

"Who won?" Tater said.

"Nobody," Wyatt said. "It was a tie, and ties are broken by the conductor. Lucille's not going to Nirvana, but Ryle's crew is." He held up his hands to quiet the chatter. "There's a fancy modern rail yard in Salt Lake. We've stopped there before, and there's still plenty of equipment for the taking. We'll stock a train for y'all to take to Nirvana, but Lucille will turn back toward Denver and keep running the loop."

"What if some of us want to go to Nirvana?" Ginny asked.

"Then you can go." Wyatt raised his voice. "We ride the train by choice. In your shoes, I'd leave, too."

"But how are we going to stock a whole other train?" Ginny asked.

"Our first step," Cheddar said, "would be to jump-start a new locomotive. We need to procure a heavy-duty pickup truck and—"

"Where's Wyatt?" Beanie burst through the door, short of breath and looking panicked. "I need to talk to him!"

The car erupted with noise.

"Beanie and Kiki get to vote, too," Ginny said.

"Not now, Ginny!" Wyatt snapped. He pushed through the riders and grabbed Beanie by the arm. "Nobody follow us," he ordered. He opened the door and pulled her through to the next car.

Beanie bent at the waist, breathing heavily. She was

winded, but it was more than that. She looked terrified.

"What's going on, Beanie?" he asked. "What did you see?"

"We rode to Cheyenne, like you said." She took another panicked breath. "Tracks are clear sailing through town, so we turned back. Then on the state line, we spotted something."

A chill ran down Wyatt's spine. *Don't tell me this, please don't tell me this.* "What was it?"

"The eastern zombie herd," she said. "Thousands and thousands spread out as far as we could see. They're coming our way."

26

RYLE

"The whole eastern zombie herd is this close to blocking our route," Wyatt told the Council in the map room "So we've got to do the turnaround faster than planned."

The train was getting close to the Wyoming state line. Across the snowy plains, the sandstone walls of Natural Fort rose up from Interstate 25. Wind whipped through the rock labyrinth, chasing snow like a broom sweeping up frosted cornflakes. Wyatt watched it, waiting for the Council to react.

"What about Beanie's and Kiki's votes?" Cheddar said. "They could swing the decision."

"They split." Wyatt shook his head. "One for, one against."

Diesel sarcastically raised his hand. "Why was I drafted for this stupid meeting?"

"You'll see," Wyatt said. "Ched, show us what you've got."

Cheddar cleared his throat and spread out a bunch of maps of Cheyenne and its rail yard. "Here's our best course of action."

Ryle made a mental checklist of his plan. Procure a heavy-duty pickup. Repair Lucille's failed second engine.

Gather supplies to stock the second train. Head back south to Denver, then west on to Salt Lake. It was fast and precise, and there was no room for error. Impressive.

After Cheddar finished, Diesel did a slow clap. "You got my vote, Cheeseboy. I volunteer to 'procure a vehicle' and make sure that it's 'well-stocked.' I could use a little joyride."

Wyatt pointed at Diesel. "You're here because we need you for this run. You get no vote on the council. Understood?"

"Joyriding is not the purpose of the pickup truck," Cheddar said. "The Salt Lake locomotive will need a jump start. For that, we need a heavy-duty pickup with a diesel engine, since we have diesel on hand."

"Diesel gets a diesel." Diesel flashed a smarmy grin. "Good call, Cheddar."

"Don't patronize me," Cheddar said as he rolled up the maps and handed them to Wyatt.

"Seriously," Diesel said. "I thought you were only good for eating your weight in Twinkies." He glared at Ryle. "You noticed how I voted on Nirvana, right?"

Ryle looked down and picked at her thumb. "My eyes were closed."

"I voted for your dumb plan," Diesel said. "Why not? We're waiting around to end up in the caboose anyway."

Ryle looked up. "What?"

"Knock it off," Wyatt said. "Meeting over."

"Finally," Diesel said. He opened a package of Snack Pack pudding. He wandered toward the dining car, probably to hold court with his crew.

Ryle cornered Wyatt at the back of the map car. "What did Diesel mean by that?"

Wyatt scrunched his eyebrows. "By what?"

"The thing with the caboose. Don't play dumb with me."

"Diesel's a jerk."

"Duh."

"He means that eventually we're all going to turn. But it's also a threat. It means you scare him." Wyatt rubbed his temple. "But in a few days, you won't have to worry about him."

"How can you be so sure?"

"Because when we reach Salt Lake, we'll get you a train to Nirvana."

"What if I don't want a train?"

Wyatt drew back, stunned. "Come again?"

"I asked you to take *all of us* to Nirvana, not dump us in Salt Lake."

"I'm—" He exhaled sharply, and a shadow of doubt crossed his face. "The conductor. I mean, compromise was the only solution. I can't risk this train for—"

"For a bunch of strandeds, right?" she said. Except Wyatt and Cheddar's plan was a good plan, and it gave them a chance without hijacking Lucille. Why did it make her so mad? "Maybe talk to Parcheesi first."

Wyatt shook his head. "Parcheesi is the last person I'm listening to."

Tell him, Ryle thought. He deserves to know. She took a deep breath. "Parcheesi is planning to hijack Lucille."

What? Wyatt mouthed the word. His face tightened in anger. "I stuck my neck out for you."

"I didn't ask you to." But she hadn't stopped him, either. "I'm sorry." Her voice cracked. "Are you going to purge us now?"

He put a finger to his lips.

She was confused. Why was he so calm? She hadn't expected that. She had to think. Had to talk Parcheesi out of the hijacking. Had to do it now, before it was too late. She ducked past Wyatt, raced from the map car and was halfway through the dining car where kids were eating, when Parcheesi burst through the opposite door.

"Hey, Parch," she said. "I was coming to—what's wrong?"

A hospital gown hung from Parcheesi's shoulder. Her hair was wild and standing on end, and her lip was pulled high above her teeth. Trickles of dark gore ran from her bloodshot eyes.

"Zombie fresh!" Diesel bellowed from behind Ryle.

Ryle barely felt the kids scramble past her. Her eyes

were locked on Parcheesi, who was taking in the air in great, ragged gulps.

Impossible, Ryle thought. I was just with her. How did she turn so fast? "Hey, Parch," she said gently. "It's going to be okay."

"It sure is," Diesel said.

He shoved Ryle aside and lunged for Parcheesi, but Parcheesi attacked impossibly fast, tearing his shirt open and knocking him down. Diesel landed on his back, and Parcheesi bit off a chunk of his ear.

"My ear!" Diesel screamed.

Gulp! Parcheesi swallowed and went for his jugular.

"No!" Ryle yelled and nailed Parcheesi with a round-house kick.

Bones cracked, and Parcheesi's head snapped back, all rage and flying spit. She vaulted into Ryle, going after her with teeth and nails. Somehow Ryle managed to roll and throw her off. She drew the bō as the zombie lowered its head to charge.

"It's me, Parch. Ryle. Friends don't eat friends."

Roar!

The zombie charged at Ryle. But its knee caught on a seat, and it stumbled, crashing into Ryle, impaling itself on the bō. Shock registered on its face, and it took Ryle down as it fell, pinning her to the floor. The zombie that had been Parcheesi didn't die gently. It scratched and snarled and spat, and no one seemed to be able to move until it took a last, wracking breath.

"Ryle!" Wyatt yelled, rolling the zombie off her.

Ryle stared at the bō like she'd never seen it before. "Not my blood," she said, gasping for air. She wiped at her eyes angrily. "I'm sorry, Wyatt. It's all my fault."

Behind her, Diesel clapped a hand over the side of his head. "Has anybody seen my ear?"

27

CHEDDAR

Cheddar watched snow fall on the prairie grass in the distance. A herd of pronghorn, *Antilocapra americana*, was grazing. Like vines and creepers, herd animals spread fast without humans to stop them. Suddenly spooked, the pronghorn bolted and disappeared.

"Knock, knock," Wyatt said, already in Cheddar's compartment. "You wanted to see me?"

"Do you gamble?"

"Weird question."

"Bear with me."

"I used to illegally buy lottery tickets at those grocery store machines."

"Did you win?"

Wyatt laughed. "Not even a dollar. The odds for that are what, one in ten?"

"Winning the jackpot was one in two billion."

Wyatt whistled.

"Why did you play with such low odds?"

"The chance at a new life." Wyatt tugged at his yellow wristband. "You know how terrible mine was."

Cheddar looked out the window at the drifting snow. "But that life had more hope than this one does."

"You think we should go to Nirvana."

"The odds of finding a cure may be small, but the payoff makes it worth buying a ticket." Cheddar paused, thinking. "Are you going to purge Ryle?"

Wyatt shook his head. "No more purging people. Even liars."

"Others abandoned me because I run like a turtle and fight like a possum." Cheddar touched his eyes, holding back tears. "You didn't."

"What loser turns his back on their one and only best friend?" Wyatt lightly punched Cheddar's shoulder. "Also, I knew you were the smartest kid in the world."

"But you won't gamble, even if the smart kid thinks Nirvana is real?"

Wyatt shook his head "If I play this wrong, we all lose our lives."

"If we don't take a chance," Cheddar said, "haven't we already lost them?"

28

WYATT

The sun had just set, and it had turned bitter cold when Lucille rolled into Cheyenne. The city had once been a major railroad hub. Lucille's second engine needed fixing, so the roundhouse machine shop would be the best place to repair it.

Only problem was that there was no direct spur to the roundhouse anymore, so Ryle and Wyatt took turns riding ahead and throwing switches. Pez navigated the rail yards flawlessly, seeming to have a sixth sense for which way they should go, even through the tangled overlapping tracks that looked like steel spaghetti.

"That's the last switch," Pez called to Ryle and Wyatt out the engineer's window. "Roundhouse is dead ahead. Somebody needs to open those big ol' doors."

"Already taken care of." Wyatt climbed to the engine deck. Luckily the snow had stopped, even though it was still icicle weather. "Sent Kiki and Beanie ahead an hour ago."

"You sent scouts alone?" Ryle asked as she swung up to the deck. "Without protection?"

"Beanie and Kiki used to be ferals," he said. "Nothing scares them."

They passed by brick buildings that were once shops and bars. Windows busted out, sidewalks littered with cars. Before the apocalypse, downtown Cheyenne had been a ghost town that underwent a revival. Now the ghosts were back. The air horn blared as Lucille veered into the round-house. Kiki and Beanie stood on either side, waving, and Wyatt felt like they'd won a small victory.

Cheddar's plan called for the scavengers to spilt into teams. Festus and Diesel, who was constantly whining about his bandaged ear, would hit the grocery. Cheddar and Vash would raid a pharmacy. Ryle and Wyatt were the truck-procuring team. In the meantime, Kiki and Beanie would keep watch, Pez would repair the second engine, and everyone else would get Lucille ready to roll.

"Okay people," Wyatt said and pulled on gloves. "Rendezvous in one hour. Don't draw attention."

Diesel and Festus took off on ATVs in a cloud of whoops and dusty snow.

"So much for not drawing attention," Wyatt muttered. He put on a motorcycle helmet. "Let's go."

They rode dirt bikes down the main street until Wyatt spotted a faded CVS sign and turned into the parking lot. "Vash, Cheddar, grab all meds that haven't been raided and anything else not nailed down."

"Meds and candy, got it." Vash parked her bike and gave

him two thumbs-up. "Where you two kids headed?"

"We're finding the truck?" Wyatt said.

Vash threw her scarf over her shoulder. "Oh, really?"

"We're finding the truck," Ryle said. "Keep those bushy brows to yourself."

Vash laughed. "Come on Ched Man. Let's score some candy!"

"Sugar is bad for your teeth," Cheddar said, cautiously getting off his dirt bike. "And must you call me Ched Man?"

"Yep," she said. "'Cause it grinds your nerves."

Cheddar dutifully followed her into the drugstore. The entrance had been smashed open. Broken glass littered the ground, and the shelves looked picked clean.

"Rendezvous in one hour," Ryle called. "Watch for zombie fresh."

"Yes, Mother!" Vash called back.

"Kids these days," Ryle said.

"They grow up so fast," Wyatt said, then fell silent as the words sunk in.

Cheddar's map showed a car dealership a couple blocks up. He pointed to a street ahead. "That's our turn."

They rode past rows of abandoned houses. The windows were all busted out. Prairie grass grew in the lawns, and ornamental trees were wrapped in climbing vines. Nature was taking over. It looked as though scavengers had stripped the stores in this neighborhood clean. They rode by what looked like a burned-out grocery store. Only the blackened shell remained, the stink of charcoal in the air.

"Scorched earth," Wyatt called to Ryle, his breath freezing in the air. "They burned it so nobody else could eat."

"Ferals aren't long-range thinkers," Ryle called back.

"You seem to know a lot about ferals," he yelled.

"You know my littles with the scars? We rescued them from ferals that had branded them with a red-hot chain. For fun. That's all I need to know about those monsters."

Wyatt was surprised that Parcheesi had rescued anyone. She'd always seemed so selfish. He turned left into the dealership. He killed the bike's engine and took off his helmet. "We need to find a diesel 4x4."

"Should be easy," Ryle said.

"Easier than getting answers from you."

"Meaning what? Are we doing this now? In the middle of a mission?"

"Seriously?" he said. "Did you plan to kill us before or after you stole the train?"

"What? No! We . . . we were going to—"

"Purge us?" he said and let her silence answer the question.

After a moment Wyatt said, "The first kid we ever purged was named Ricky. He was turning, but it was too soon. After we pushed him off, he shambled after the train, but we left him behind. He was one of . . . he was a friend."

"I'm sorry, Wyatt."

"We learned—"

"Not about him, well, about him, too, but about the train jacking plan. For lying to you. I didn't know."

"It's okay," he said. How do you explain that you'd do the same thing to survive? "I get it."

"Do you? Really?"

"I do. Really."

She sighed. Waited. Thought. "Why don't you, y'know?"

"Put them down?" He looked up at the sky which, bizarrely, was still blue. "Seems more humane, doesn't it? But we can't. Because there's always the chance they might never turn all the way."

"Dude, hate to break it to you," she said, "but everybody turns."

29

WYATT

Wyatt and Ryle hid the dirt bikes in tall grass next to the car lot. Before they had crossed the pavement, a loud crack filled the air. Ryle drew her bō, and Wyatt stepped in front of her, paintball gun ready.

"See anything?" she asked.

"Let's keep moving," he said.

They jogged until they reached the showroom. It was ruined. Smashed-out windows. Graffiti on every wall. The ferals had left their mark.

"What brings you in today, pardna?" Ryle asked in a TV salesman voice. "Can I interest you in a zero-interest, zero-payment loan? Good on any vehicle on the lot."

Wyatt snorted.

"That's all I get?" she asked.

He grinned.

She grinned back.

"Where would they keep the keys?" said Wyatt.

Ryle pointed at the sales manager's office. "Start there."

The office was what Wyatt expected. Stained and moldy carpet. A dust-covered desk. Dead plants. Contracts awaiting signatures. A safety glass window overlooking the showroom.

"Clear," Wyatt said.

Ryle walked around the desk. "Somebody beat us to the key safe."

The keys were strewn over the moldy carpet, the serial numbers on the tags almost too faded to read.

She sorted through them. "For my sweet sixteen," she said, "I want a red Miata convertible with white leather seats. You?"

Wyatt squatted beside her. Group homes didn't celebrate birthdates or holidays. All he'd ever wished was that he and Pike would be a family again. "Mustang."

"Hmm." Ryle cut her eyes at him. "Always saw you as a Prius kind of guy."

"Very funny. Here's one," Wyatt said. "How about a Silverado?"

"Gas engine," she said. "We need a diesel."

He tossed the keys. "Good point."

"Ah ha!" Ryle swooped up a fob. "Ford F-250 diesel—look out!"

Whomp!

Something slammed into the window overlooking the showroom.

A girl.

Her sallow face was pressed against the glass, her hands smeared with something gooey and brown.

Ryle covered her mouth. "What's on her face?"

"Looks like chocolate."

A Hershey's wrapper was clenched in her fist. Behind her, a metal accordion gate separated a break room from the vending machines. The machines were smashed, every candy bar and bag of chips gone. Crumpled wrappers covered the floor. Apparently the girl had found the last chocolate bar.

She'd also found herself a zombie fresh. It was almost six feet tall with wild blond hair, and it was trying to claw through the accordion gate slats, desperate for its own snack.

The gate was unlatched. The zombie was coming. The girl hammered furiously on the glass.

Ryle motioned for the girl to duck. "Cover your eyes!"

The girl blinked twice, her face a question mark.

"Cover your—never mind." Ryle shattered the glass with her bō, and a half second later the window fell. The crash filled the room, and the chocolate-faced girl covered her ears.

Ryle jumped through the window and rushed to the accordion gate.

"Watch out!" Wyatt yelled as he followed.

The gate swung open abruptly. The zombie staggered through. Wyatt brought the gun up and *thwip-thwip*! Put paintballs in the zombie's eyeballs. The zombie slammed into the wall and collapsed.

"He was my friend," the girl gasped as Wyatt reached for her. "But he was going to eat me."

"I'm sorry," Wyatt said.

The girl wrapped her arms around Wyatt. "Thanks for saving me."

Maybe not so sorry, Wyatt thought as he peeled her off. Her arms were a vice grip, and whoa, she smelled as sour as she looked. Wyatt guessed a month since her last bath.

Ryle looked down at her. "What's your story?"

"Stories are for babies and suckers," the girl said, sneering.

"Are you hurt?" Wyatt asked.

The girl stuck out her arm. Deep bite marks covered her forearm. The wounds were crusted with scabs. "I'm going to turn now."

"That's not how it works." Ryle looked at Wyatt. "Everything you know about zombies is wrong."

Wyatt smiled.

"Bobby said to kill zombies," the girl said, "you have to bash their skulls and scramble their brains like eggs."

"Who's Bobby?"

She pointed to the zombie slumped on the floor.

"Bobby was wrong," Wyatt said. "And he's not dead."

"So you can still scramble his brains," the girl said, clapping.

"Um, no," Wyatt said. "But your bite might be infected,

so we need to clean it. A bath wouldn't hurt, either."

The girl's face puckered. "What're you trying to say?"

"We've got company," Ryle said.

Five shamblers in business suits lurched through the hallway door next to the vending machines. They shuffled slowly, throats clicking. The lead shambler was bloated, its puffy neck garroted by a striped tie. Its belly bulged around its belt, and it looked like a prime candidate to go Dumpty.

Five zombies was bad news, but shamblers were easy to outrun. "Let's go," Wyatt said. "Still got that key?"

Ryle shook the fob. "Your dream pumpkin awaits."

"Check the office door," he told Ryle.

Ryle held up a finger for quiet, then jumped back quickly. She shook her head. "Hallway to the showroom is full."

"Okay," he said, "let's pause a second to—"

Ryle swung the door open and charged into the hallway, screaming bloody murder. Wyatt grabbed the girl's hand and started after. He headed for the fire exit, but a shambler in a white silk blouse and navy skirt came at them with outstretched arms and bright blue fingernails. It grabbed the girl by the hair.

"Ow!" the girl yelled. "Leggo!"

Wyatt stuck the paintball gun in the zombie's armpit. "Nice manicure," he said, pulling the trigger. The high-pressured paintball separated the zombie's rotted arm from the shoulder, its fingers still wrapped in the girl's hair.

The girl's scream could curdle milk. "Get it off! Get it off!"

"Hold still!" Wyatt said, twisting the zombie arm free.

The zombie poked at its empty shoulder socket as more shamblers packed the hallway. Wyatt fired paintballs *thwip-thwip-thwip* at the pack, and they fell back onto the others, taking them down like bowling pins.

"Catch!" Wyatt said and tossed the arm on the pile.

Two shamblers grabbed it and started a tug of war. It would've been funny if the arm hadn't been, well, an arm.

"That'll slow them down," he said, then called, "Ryle!"

"This way!" Ryle said, hitting the fire exit door. "Hurry up, slackers!"

Finally outside in the lot, Wyatt turned in circles, the girl still clinging to him. It would take forever to find the F250.

Ryle held up the key fob and hit the panic button. The alarm let off a booming *whoop-whoop*, and a bar of lights flashed manically. "There!" She pointed across the snowy lot. "Hey, it really is a pumpkin."

A crew cab with a bar of hunting lights on top. Fog lights in front. A massive whip antenna on the bumper. Painted fluorescent orange and blue with a bucking bronco on the hood. Ryle hit the button to unlock the doors. The alarm fell silent as shamblers spilled from the showroom and into the lot. Dozens now, coming from everywhere.

"Brrr!" the girl cried out. "It's colder than a penguin's butt out here!"

Wyatt handed her his coat and swung the rear door open. He deposited the girl in the crew cab. "Keys," he said to Ryle.

"A Y chromosome makes you a better driver?"

"Chromosomes, schmosomes. I've got the best reflexes."

"Yet I took out a dozen zombies while you snuggled a little girl."

"Good point," he said and swept snow off the windshield. "Get us out of here before the vampire cows stampede."

"Vampire . . . " She smiled. "You know, I actually got that. What about our dirt bikes?"

"Forget the bikes for now." Wyatt jumped in the passenger seat. "Buckle up," he told the girl.

Ryle turned the ignition, and the massive diesel engine clattered to life. The sound system boomed "Sabotage." Wyatt reached for the volume. Ryle knocked his hand away and slammed the accelerator. Their heads slapped the headrests, and the truck roared through the lot.

With a quick turn of the wheel, Ryle made the rear end whipsaw, taking three shamblers out at the knees. "Youth bowling league champion three years running," she said and laid rubber. "Next stop, Nirvana!"

30

RYLE

As the truck peeled from the dealership lot, Ryle danced in her seat. Wyatt let out a horse laugh, then covered his mouth, embarrassed, and Ryle giggled uncontrollably as she made a hard right turn. The rear end fishtailed, and she lost control, doing an ice-aided one-eighty in the middle of Main Street.

"Oops," she said. It felt good to laugh, a real laugh, not a forced one to make others feel better. She hit the gas, and they shot down the road, dodging wreckage like a two-ton slalom skier on tricked-out skis.

Wyatt turned in the seat. "Sometimes you have to laugh at the scary stuff."

In the rearview, the girl stared at Ryle blankly. There was something different about her eyes—they were distant, a little cold. She didn't look so innocent now.

"How old are you?" Ryle asked.

The girl stared back at Ryle. "Fourteen."

Fourteen? Ryle thought. Nobody was fourteen freaking years old. She had to be lying.

"But you're so short," Wyatt said.

"I'm five foot one, dork. Not my fault you and your girl-friend are Amazons."

"No offense," Wyatt said. "But if you're fourteen—let me see your fingers."

The girl held up two middle fingers. "How's that?"

"Her nails are black," Wyatt said. "All of them."

Ryle slammed the brakes. Black fingernails were usually the first sign of the change, followed by bloodshot eyes. She turned to face the girl, whose eyes were clear. "But you haven't turned?"

"Obviously," the girl said.

"You should be a zombie," Wyatt said. "Why aren't you?"

"Because I've never been bit before." She held up her arm with the teeth marks in it. "How long does it take?"

"You don't get the parasite from zombie bites," said Ryle.

"We don't know what triggers it," Wyatt said. "When did your nails turn black?"

"A year ago?" The girl rolled her eyes. "What difference does it make?"

"Because," Wyatt said, "maybe you're never going to turn. What's your name?"

"Starla," she said.

"Come back with us," Ryle said. "We can get you food, a hot shower, and meds for the bite. Right, Wyatt?"

"Not interested," said Starla, reaching for the door handle. "Drop me off on the next corner."

Ryle traded a nod with Wyatt. There was probably an

immune person right in their truck, and she been holed up in a car dealership living off vending machines. They couldn't let the girl go, even if it meant keeping her against her will. It meant they'd be kidnappers. But if it saved all of them and even the whole human race, what choice did they have?

"Shut the door," Ryle said and felt guilt tighten her chest.

"Sorry, Starla," Wyatt said, aiming the paintball gun at her. "You're coming with us."

31

DIESEL

It was pitch-dark when Festus stumbled from Lucky's Market, arms loaded with breakfast cereals. He navigated an icy path littered with broken glass until he reached two shopping carts and dropped the boxes atop the rest of their haul. Most of it was canned goods. A few packets of instant breakfast, sports drinks, and assorted cake mixes.

"Pick up the pace!" Diesel sat on the curb, eating the last Twinkie from a box Festus had found. The cold made his ear throb, even through the bandages. Not that anybody cared. "The dorks'll be back soon."

"We aren't sharing the Twinkies?" Festus asked.

"I gave you one." Diesel picked up a cereal box. He ripped the top off and shook Shredded Wheat onto the cracked asphalt. "No secret toy surprise. What a rip-off."

Festus blinked at him. "You didn't save none for me?"

"What?" He ripped open a second box. "I hate Shredded Wheat. Cap'n Crunch. Now that's a meal for a man. Find some."

"Ain't no Cap'n inside. All the good stuff's gone."

"Go look anyway."

Festus blinked again. "Why're you always mean to me, Big D?"

"Stop slobbering." Diesel fired a wheat biscuit at Festus. It bounced off his forehead. "You going to cry again? *It's hard to do this stuff by myself! It's dark in there.* Wah-wah-wah. If I'd known you were such a baby, I'd let the zombies eat you."

"That hurt my feelings," Festus said and wiped his nose with his dirty sleeve.

"Disgusting!" Diesel threw a second biscuit, then another. "Get outta my face."

Festus put his head down and hurried back inside the grocery.

"Dork!" Diesel laughed, then stuffed the last Twinkie into his mouth. What a moron. Once he became conductor, Festus was going to get purged with the other losers.

"You stole that delicious sponge cake you're spitting on."

Diesel stopped chewing and glanced over his shoulder. A boy. Younger than he was. Under a tree about twenty feet away. Diesel reached for the multi-tool he'd clipped to his belt.

The kid raised an aluminum bat. "Don't even think about it."

Four more boys appeared. All with wild hair caked with mud and brands on their cheeks. Ferals, Diesel thought.

"You took something from Lich," the first boy said, walking toward Diesel. He plucked the sponge cake from Diesel's fingers, then put the bat barrel under his chin.

"It's a freaking Twinkie, bruh," Diesel said, his Adam's apple bumping the freezing cold bat.

"This ain't about the Twinkie," the boy said. "You people took something, and Lich wants it back."

"I don't—"

"Liars get lickins." The boy pushed the bat against Diesel's bandaged ear. "Don't lie to us, Diesel."

Diesel winced. "How do you know my name?"

"We know everything. There's you two here at the store. A fat boy and a girl with a mohawk at the drugstore. A tall boy and a girl with purple hair driving a truck here to give you a ride, since y'all's ATVs got stolen."

"But my ATV is parked right over there. Oh."

"Don't feel bad. We stole all the dirt bikes, too." The feral boy spat through the gaps in his teeth. "Help us fetch what the tall boy stole, and Lich'll give you a reward."

"What did the idiot steal this time?" Diesel said. "And what if I say no?"

"Your mouth might say no." The boy grinned. "But my bat says yes. So listen up. This's how it's going down."

32

WYATT

Five minutes later the bright orange F-250 pulled into the CVS parking lot, and Wyatt unbuckled his seat belt. On the way back, he could feel eyes everywhere, tracking them in the dark. Maybe it was guilt. Ryle said kidnapping Starla was the lesser of two evils, but even though he agreed, it didn't sit right with him.

Ryle stopped the truck and hit the horn. "Don't budge," she told Starla. "And don't try anything funny."

Starla stared at Wyatt with pleading eyes. "Come on, Wyatt, don't let her treat me like this," she said. "I'll go with you if you got food and stuff, but it ain't fair to go cutting into me."

"Nobody's going to hurt you," he said, "but like Ryle said—no funny business." He turned and yelled out his window. "Hey guys! Let's go!"

Cheddar and Vash stepped into the headlight beams with overloaded shopping bags and overstuffed backpacks. They laughed and joked, chewing on strips of beef jerky. Vash swigged an orange soda.

"Dude," Vash said and stopped short. "Where are the bikes?"

"Forget the bikes," Wyatt called. "Just get in."

Starla started pounding on the rear window. "Help me! I got bit by zombies, and now they want to dissect me!"

"That sounds unlikely," said Cheddar, loading their bags in the back of the truck.

"Whoa," Vash said, doing a double take. "Who's the hitchhiker?"

Ryle unlocked the doors. "Guys, meet Marla—"

"It's Starla!"

"—the oldest girl in the world."

"Don't you mean the stinkiest girl in the world?" Vash scrunched up her nose as she climbed into the backseat. "Dang, don't you bathe?"

Starla fired a fist that caught Vash square in the eye. The orange soda fell and shattered on the pavement. Vash slapped a hand over her eye, tears streaming down her cheeks.

"My Fanta!" Vash raised a fist. "You little—"

"No hitting, Vash!" Ryle reached back and caught Vash's hand. "Carla's fourteen, and her nails are completely black. Get me? She agreed to come with us. To Nirvana."

"I ain't agreed to nothing," Starla argued. "And stop messing up my name."

Cheddar climbed into the backseat behind Wyatt. "You think she has something to do with Nirvana? What is your theory?"

"Once we're back at the roundhouse," Wyatt said, "I'll figure it out."

"Figure it out fast," Vash said, her eye quickly swelling. "So I can hit Marla back."

"It's Starla," said the girl, keeping far away from Vash, who pulled licorice whips, like long red shoelaces, from her backpack.

"Don't be eyeing my licorice, stinky," Vash said, turning away.

"You've got no right to do this," Starla said as they started out of the parking lot. "Taking me away from my home. Away from my boyfriend, who I love with all my heart."

"I doubt that."

"That I've got a boyfriend?"

"That you've got a heart," Ryle said.

"Lich ain't going to like this," Starla said.

"Who's Lich?" Wyatt asked.

"Lich's my boyfriend," Starla said, "and he's going to be really, really mad. A really, really mad Lich is a really—"

But Wyatt lost her last words in the roar of an ATV that shot past them. The driver was a girl, and she was definitely not Diesel.

33

WYATT

The Cheyenne Union Pacific Roundhouse looked like a Parmesan cheese wheel cut down the middle, with engine repair chambers that resembled mouseholes. The floors were cement, the walls red brick. Floor-to-ceiling glass and steel windows. Steel girders created catwalks to reach the second and third floors. On the third floor the two outriders, Beanie and Kiki, kept watch. They walked the circular catwalk, using high-powered binoculars to scout downtown Cheyenne.

Tater's little ones had to uncouple each car and spin it on the turntable When Lucille was repaired, they would roll her from the mouseholes, spin her around, then couple everything. It was a long and hard process. So Wyatt was surprised that the job looked about eighty percent complete. Only the boxcars and caboose were left.

Just after nine p.m., Ryle drove the pickup truck into the roundhouse and parked next to the flatcar. They all jumped out, Ryle pulling Starla behind her.

Wyatt waved Tater over and tossed him the keys. "Park the truck in the flatcar. We'll be right back."

"Where's the ATVs and dirt bikes?" Tater said, shivering despite his down coat.

"We lost them," Wyatt said. "Store the truck and move the supplies to the boxcars. Cheddar, Diesel, and Festus will help."

Diesel snorted. "I got things to do, *Conductor*."

"Like cleaning latrines. But that can wait," Wyatt said. "Ryle, Vash, and Starla. Come with me."

"I ain't going nowhere," Starla said, turning to run.

Ryle caught her by the collar. "Sure you are."

"Lay off!" Starla yelled and sank her teeth into Ryle's arm.

"You bit me!" She shook Starla but didn't let go. "You little brat!"

"It barely broke the skin," she said, "and that's what you get for treating me like garbage."

With Starla protesting, they walked across the tracks to the mousehole where Pez was still working on Lucille. Wyatt could smell the grease in the air. The sound of hammers and heavy machinery echoed through the steel and brick-framed windows.

"What's the story?" he asked Pez.

The engineer was covered in grease, and he looked as happy as a pig in mud. "She's been worse," he said and gave a rundown. They'd stabilized engine one, but they had really only slapped a Band-Aid on it. "Both engines will run as long as she only has to walk."

A shrill whistle sounded, and Kiki yelled, "Wyatt! Up

here!" from her perch on the third floor catwalk. She held up the night-vision binoculars. "Come take a look!"

What now? Wyatt thought.

He ran up to the third floor and took the binoculars from Kiki. He scanned all directions, spotting ghostly gray shapes against the black background of the buildings. Zombies. Hundreds of them jam-packing the roads surrounding the rail yard.

"Shamblers," Wyatt said.

"Yup," Kiki said. "The great eastern herd."

"Son of a biscuit eater," he said. "Grab your bikes. We need y'all to guide the train out." Then he yelled down to the riders, "Listen up people, our timeline's changed! Let's pack it up and move out!"

"Pez," Wyatt asked. "You've got all the cars coupled right? Everything's good to pull out? Why isn't the engine running?"

Pez was frantically throwing the start switch on the locomotive's control board. "This thing is giving me fits," Pez said. "Can't start Lucille too fast or her pistons might seize."

"I can help Pez with Lucille," Vash said.

Pez glowered. "Lucille's got all the help she can stand."

"Obviously not, or engine one would be running." Vash

pushed Pez aside and threw the switch. The engine fired. "Voilà! Easy-peasy."

"Of course it was easy," Pez complained. "Any dummy could just throw the start switch. I was trying to ease her into it."

"Nice work, Vash," Wyatt said. "After Lucille warms up, get her up to ten mph."

Pez shook his head. "That might be suicide."

"Ours?"

"Lucille's."

"Remember how I said there's a zombie herd?" asked Wyatt.

"Six miles per hour. Any more'n that, and Lucille's liable to—"

"Blow us to smithereens, right." Wyatt patted Pez's shoulder. "Ten mph. ASAP. In the meantime, there's a guest I've got to welcome to the train."

Wyatt prodded Starla into a cell at the back of the second passenger car. He closed the door and locked it. Starla was facing the wall when he dropped the key into his pocket.

"This is where they went?" she said. "Into a cage. Like a dog."

"Where who went?" he asked, staring at her through the porthole window. She wasn't making any sense.

"The kids," she said. "Parcheesi's kids. Your kids. Mixed together like the freaking Brady Bunch. It'd be a lovely story if it weren't for one thing." Then she laughed. "We wondered when they all disappeared."

"We who? What are you talking about?"

"Your big happy family's all alone in the world," she told the wall. "The rest is ferals and zombies, and the zombies are winning."

"That's not true."

"Ask Ryle. She's seen it herself. I can tell by the look in her eyes. The zombies are hungry," she said, smirking, "and your brains are what's for dinner."

From the passenger car, Wyatt thumbed the PA mic and ordered the water cannon installed in the bed of the bright orange truck. Then he called for Ryle to meet him at the flatbed car. In the minutes it took to haul out and mount the cannon to the truck, Wyatt ran up and down the train cars, getting riders aboard, calling lookouts back, making sure nobody got left behind.

"Riders!" he called over the noise. "Don't stand there with your tongues hanging out! Let's move!"

Seconds later Ryle fell in beside him, matching him stride for stride. "The water cannon is portable?" she said. "And you didn't tell me?"

"Because I knew you'd want to shoot it."

"It's a cannon! Of course I would!" Then she grinned. "Want to drive this time? I shouldn't hog all the fun."

Wyatt grinned back. "Ever shot a water cannon before?"

"Do video games count?"

"Yeah, but no. Grabbing the handles of a cannon is like grabbing a bighorn sheep in one hand and a mountain lion in another."

"I have experience wrestling wild animals."

"You do not."

"Neither do you, which makes us even. I'm taking the water cannon!"

34

WYATT

A moment later Pez hit the air horn, and Lucille slowly, achingly pulled forward, leaving the roundhouse behind. The train's massive headlights lit the dark track as the train gained speed, with Beanie and Kiki riding point on their dirt bikes and Wyatt and Ryle in the truck protecting Lucille's flanks.

"Test round!" Ryle yelled through the cab's sliding rear window. She fired on a sidewalk sculpture of a cowboy boot. Water jets tore at the fiberglass in a wild and furious pattern, and the boot disintegrated. "Whoa! This baby's got some kick."

"Thought you'd like it!" Wyatt called from the cab.

The tracks headed due west, so Wyatt cut a wide circle across the labyrinth of steel toward the railroad museum. The parking lot was filled with blown sand, litter, dead tree limbs, and zombies. When the sound of Lucille's engine reached them, they turned like a school of fish noticing a baited hook.

"Come to mama!" Ryle yelled, gripping the handles of the cannon tightly.

Wyatt looked back at Ryle. Though she was firing zingers, her face looked tense and afraid. For some reason, it made him relax knowing that she was scared, too. "Wait till you see the yellow of their teeth, Ryle!"

"What if they don't have any teeth?"

"Wait till you can see their gums!"

She laughed as he steered closer, putting the truck between the parking lot and Lucille as the train navigated the spaghetti maze of tracks and switches.

"Gums!" Wyatt yelled when a zombie fresh blasted through the herd. It wore a battered tuxedo with a shredded cummerbund and had a dirt-encrusted beard and a bald head covered in scabs.

"Look!" Ryle called. "This one's dressed to kill!"

She waited till it lurched onto the truck bed. She squeezed the trigger, and the zombie disintegrated in front of her.

"Double whoa!" she cackled.

Wyatt yanked the wheel to the left and gunned it, fishtailing loose dirt behind the truck. Ryle was acting weird. Something had changed, and he didn't know what it was. No time to stop and think about it, though, so he pulled slowly alongside Lucille, the truck bouncing over the railroad ties.

"Save some water for later," he yelled back to her. "The tank's not bottomless."

She stopped firing as the caboose cleared the last switch and left the yard. "All clear!" she yelled.

Wyatt felt himself relax a little as Lucille picked up speed, but then they rounded the museum and a wave of zombies came from nowhere. In a heartbeat, the once-empty streets were awash in a nightmare. Shamblers poured from the alleys like a flooded river overflowing a dam.

"Hey, uglies!" Wyatt yelled and blasted the horn hard, trying to draw their attention.

The shamblers turned as one and crashed against the truck cab, slamming the glass from the passenger window. They pummeled the bed and rattled the tailgate.

"Hang tight!" he yelled to Ryle and gunned it.

Tires spun and threw smoke behind them, thick with the stink of burning rubber. Wyatt swerved hard to the right, slamming shamblers against a brick wall, and he didn't let up, pushing the truck hard to the left, then snapping back to the right and plowing through more shamblers.

Ryle blasted the zombies climbing over each other to get to her. "Eat it!" she screamed.

When Wyatt looked back at the road, a snarling zombie was clinging to the hood and clawing its way to the windshield.

"Hold on!" he shouted, hitting the brakes.

Ryle slammed into the sliding window, and Wyatt felt her hand on his shoulder.

"Scoot over!" Ryle shouted. "Let me drive!"

"No way! I'm in the middle of something!"

"The middle of getting us killed!" She climbed into the cab. "Go take the cannon. I've got the wheel."

Wyatt had barely climbed through the window when Ryle slammed the truck into four-wheel drive, steered away from the tracks, then gunned it over a gully.

With a roar, the truck bounced into the air, front wheels spinning.

"Keep the wheels on the—oof!—ground!" Wyatt yelled. "Make zombies follow you!"

The engine roared again. The wheels hit the ground. Ryle whipped around in a tight three-sixty, then slammed the brakes.

The headlights lit up the dust cloud she'd made. She flashed the high beams repeatedly, then laid on the horn.

"Not working," she yelled. "Any bright ideas?"

"Just one!" Wyatt yelled back.

Wyatt pulled the trigger and unleashed a high-pressure torrent of water. The blast hit the shamblers like a wall, and they were blown backward. But then three zombie fresh broke free of the writhing clump and made a frantic blood-thirsty rush for the truck. Wyatt swung the cannon at the lead fresh. The jets hit it square in the teeth and spun it around like a merry-go-round on ice.

"Floss that!" he yelled. "Ryle! Zombie fresh! Blind them!"

Ryle flashed the high beams. "It's daylight, dummy!"

"Doesn't matter!" Wyatt banged on the roof. "Keep the lights on!"

Ryle backed onto the sidewalk. Shamblers stumbled toward the retreating truck, and their herky-jerky movements sent them tumbling into the gully, but they didn't stay down long. They used one another's heads as stepping stones and crawled their way out.

"It's working!" Wyatt yelled. "Keep going!"

Then the ground disappeared under the back wheels.

"Ditch!" he yelled and grabbed the light bar for balance. "Cut to the right!"

Ryle yanked the wheel hard. "Hold on!"

The truck pounded over a concrete berm and tilted at a sharp angle. The right wheels dug into the snow, and the left front spat chunks at the relentless herd.

Wyatt took aim. Three rotten melon heads popped as a skinny zombie fresh with a rat's nest of dusted black hair launched itself at the front fender. Its claws latched onto the grill, and it scrambled over the hood.

Wyatt squeezed the trigger, but the cannon was dry. "Hitchhiker! Reverse!"

"Can't you blast it?"

"Tank's empty!"

Ryle slammed into reverse and gunned the engine. The truck rocketed downhill, bucked the hitchhiker off, and barreled through the line of shamblers.

"Granny on our six!" Ryle yelled.

Wyatt turned to see a zombie granny climbing over the icy tailgate. Short, skeletally thin, with salt-and-pepper hair. It reached for Wyatt. Hands out and dentures clacking.

Wyatt drop-kicked it back over the tailgate. The dentures hit the truck bed, and he scooped them up. "Got your teeth!"

The truck hit a snow mound, and Wyatt tumbled over the tailgate. He landed on the asphalt. Hard. He wheezed for air.

The truck veered into the herd as the zombie granny screamed then lunged for its dentures. "Teef! Teef!"

Wyatt sidestepped it in the nick of time. Then he realized—it had just spoken words. A zombie was talking! "You want teeth?" He threw the dentures. "Take 'em!"

They bounced off the granny's forehead. Zombie fresh were fast but not coordinated. She stumbled ahead, arms outstretched. "Teef! Teef!" She grabbed the dentures and tried to shove them in her mouth.

Wyatt laughed at how silly she looked. Until she growled and charged at him.

He went for a hip shot.

The paintball gun clicked empty.

"Mother of pearl."

Granny fresh nailed him with a tackle, and they rolled

across the pavement, Granny holding the dentures while vainly gumming his forearm through his coat. In that moment he wondered about its yearning to get its teeth back. Was part of its lizard brain intact? If a granny zombie could talk—and think—what about the others? Were they more than just mindless vampire cows roaming the countryside?

As possibilities raced through his mind, the granny lost her grip, and he was back on his feet. Zombie Granny snarled a deep, guttural "Teef," lunging for him as a horn sounded. Then Granny snorked in surprise and looked up, just as the bumper of the orange truck slammed into her hip.

Granny zombie went flying.

So did the dentures.

Ryle whistled, and the truck door flew open. "Don't stand there catching flies. Get in!" she yelled.

He jumped in. "Nice takedown."

Ryle hit the accelerator. "Where to?"

"Let's get away from here," Wyatt said. He wanted to ask her about the granny zombie. See what she thought. If the zombies could talk and think, maybe they weren't brainless after all. Did that make them less dangerous? Or even more deadly?

"Shamblers on my rear!" Ryle yelled.

Wyatt looked in the side mirror. A picket line of twenty

shamblers was converging on the truck. "Take it easy," he said. "You can't plow through them. Too much mass."

Ryle hit the gas. "Buckle up, buttercup."

"Do not. Do this."

The engine roared. Ryle did, too. A gap opened in the herd, and Ryle veered toward it. "Brace! Brace! Cover your eyes!"

Ryle threw an arm over her face, and Wyatt wrapped an arm around her. The truck plowed straight through the shamblers. Wyatt opened his eyes. The truck was covered with Dumpty goo.

"I see the train!" Wyatt shouted, pointing at the red caboose disappearing in the distance. A surge of adrenaline hit him. "Don't let Lucille get away!"

"Dude, a little trust here?"

The truck tires skidded on the snowy pavement as Ryle jumped the embankment. Wyatt's teeth chattered as the big tires pounded the railroad ties, and zombies fell away to the right and left. Ryle drove off the rails and onto the railbed.

Then there was blessed silence.

Ryle drove hard ahead and caught up with Lucille quickly. When they reached the second boxcar, she sounded the horn three times to signal the kids on the flatcar to drop the hydraulic lift.

"We won!" Ryle cheered as she steered onto the ramp.

"We won," Wyatt said and felt an intense rush of relief. The worst part was over. They had escaped by the skin of their teeth, but Lucille was moving, and they had left the herd in their wake.

It was all downhill from here.

He hoped.

35

WYATT

After they parked the truck on the flatcar, Ryle killed the engine and tossed Wyatt the keys. He let out a sigh. That was too close. They had barely escaped with their lives, even with the cannon. What would they do if the herd surrounded Lucille?

"You okay?" he asked her. Ryle was hiding something. He could feel it.

"Just got the shakes," Ryle said, "probably from the adrenaline rush."

"Good," he replied, though he wasn't reassured.

"Cleanup on aisle whatever," Vash's voice squawked over the PA. "There's zombies attacking the caboose. Can a girl get some help?"

"No rest for the weary," Ryle said, jumping from the truck. "You coming or not?"

What choice was there? "Right behind you," he said.

They quickly reached the caboose and joined Vash on the roof. The cold wind whipped through her hair, and she was loading two paintball guns in the moonlight.

"What's the situation, Vash?" Ryle asked.

"Situation's we're being followed by hungry zombies.

What else is new?" Vash passed a paintball gun to Ryle as a zombie poked its head over the roof of the caboose, looking in the opposite direction. "I was chilling till the cavalry got here. But y'all will do. Get it, y'all will do? Why ain't you laughing, Ryle?"

"'Cause you're not funny," Ryle said. "And we've got a visitor."

The zombie turned toward them. It jerked with surprise, as if it had just spotted them, and awkwardly climbed onto the roof.

"Fire away," Wyatt said, loading his own gun with Vash's paintballs. "But we don't have unlimited ammo, so aim for the eyes."

Vash fired paintballs *thwip-thwip-thwip* into the eyes of the zombie fresh, which clawed its face, stumbled sideways, and fell off the caboose.

"Timber!" Vash yelled.

"Seriously." Ryle shook her head. "Your sense of humor is completely demented."

"Best compliment ever." Vash laughed. "Coming from a girl who thinks puns are funny."

"They're hilarious."

"I think you mean painful."

"Whoa, what's that noise?" Wyatt yelled. "Listen!"

There was a loud clank and a *whump*, and Wyatt felt a jolt shoot through the caboose, followed by the sensation of letting go. The caboose jerked again, throwing them all to their knees.

"Dude," Vash said, shaking her head. "What hit us? A train-hating bison?"

Wyatt crawled to the edge and looked down at the source of the clanking noise. "Oh, no." It was worse than getting T-boned by a buffalo. The caboose was completely uncoupled from the car ahead. Only a safety chain connected the two cars, and the chain was bucking and groaning, sounding like it might snap at any second.

"We've got trouble!" He stood and grabbed Vash's shoulder. "The coupling's failed. We've got to jump for it. Now!"

Vash stopped laughing. "What?"

Ryle looked at the growing gap between the train and the caboose and didn't hesitate. "Let's go!" She took a running start and leapt, landing safely on the flatcar. "Vash! Jump. Now!"

Vash followed hard on her heels. "Made it!"

Ryle stuck out a hand to Wyatt. "Jump!"

He shook his head. "I can't leave them behind."

"Them? I thought the caboose was empty," she said and put a hand over her mouth as she seemed to realize something. "Vash!" she yelled. "That heavy chain hanging on the lift! Throw it to me! We've got to save the caboose!"

The freezing wind whipped her hair across her face, and her eyes were hidden by darkness, but Wyatt could still feel her gaze. *She understood.* Then she caught the heavy chain from Vash and started gathering it to throw to him.

Whump!

The safety chain suddenly snapped—a quick, hard sound like a gunshot. Wyatt heard metal strike metal as the broken chain recoiled. The train shuddered, a violent, brief force, enough to knock him flat onto the metal roof.

Then there was silence like the gasp of a final breath, and Wyatt crawled to the edge of the car. He looked down at the failed coupling. A cold shiver ran down his spine.

The coupling hadn't failed.

Somebody had lifted the pin and separated the cars.

On purpose.

36

WYATT

"Somebody lifted the pin!" Wyatt yelled as Ryle and Vash threw the heavy chain across the gap between cars.

"Tie it off on the ladder!" Ryle yelled after he'd grabbed it. "You're running out of time—look out!"

Wyatt turned to see the dark shapes of two zombies climbing the ladder to the roof of the caboose. He strafed their faces with paintballs, and they tumbled backward. A third zombie popped up. Wyatt took it out with one shot, and it fell. He was about to reload when the caboose jerked again, and he fell to his knees.

That's what zombies do, Wyatt thought. They keep coming no matter what, right in your face. People waited till your back was turned to attack. Someone had pulled the pin. Was it to get rid of him? Or the caboose?

"Don't just stand there! Tie the chain off!" Ryle yelled.

Wyatt knotted the chain around the ladder three times, rust coating his hands. The chain caught, and the caboose lurched. Wheels groaned. The ladder rung bent. The chain slacked again and tightened again and slacked again.

Wyatt fell back onto the caboose roof. The paintball gun slipped from his cold hand and slid away. He dived for it and snagged it before it disappeared into the frigid night, but his momentum almost sent him over the edge.

"Grab onto something!" Ryle called.

"I'm trying!" he yelled back and caught hold of a vent pipe.

A zombie, a one-eyed zombie fresh, vaulted up the rear ladder and dropped beside him. *"Gnar!"*

"Gnar to you, too!" Wyatt yelled.

The fresh bellowed and grabbed Wyatt's hand. It opened its rotting maw to take a bite, and Wyatt rammed the paint gun barrel into its mouth. Teeth crunched as it tried to chew through the metal pipe, and Wyatt pulled the trigger. A paintball fired into the fresh's mouth, and its eyes went wide. It made a noise like *snert* and gagged. Blue paint flew from the corners of its mouth as Wyatt grabbed its beard, spun to one knee, and flipped it off the caboose.

"The one almost goateed you!" Vash yelled. "Get it? Goateed you? 'Cause he has a beard?"

Wyatt gave Ryle a shaky thumbs-up and sat down. It was almost too much to deal with. He was only twelve.

"Why are you still sitting there?" Ryle called. "Jump! We need you over here!"

"I can't!" he yelled.

"What do you mean you can't?" Vash yelled back. "Get a running start and just jump. Ain't nothing stopping you!"

But there was. Somebody had tried to dump the caboose. He wanted to know who lifted the pin, and the nurse might have seen something.

He stood and scrambled down to the front of the caboose. "I have to go inside!"

Vash turned to Ryle. "Has that boy lost his mind?"

"I don't get it," Ryle called as the train sped up. "Who's in there?"

Wyatt started climbing down the ladder to the vestibule. "The old Council," he yelled and every word felt heavy. "What's left of it."

WYATT

A moment later Wyatt pounded on the red door. "Bed check!"

The door swung halfway open, and Wyatt slipped inside. The dust-covered windows were intact, but the rear door was wrecked. Moonlight seeped through the broken glass, shards jutting from the window frame. They dripped with the dark, thick blood of zombie fresh.

"That's your doing?" Wyatt asked the nurse.

The nurse smiled a little bit, a rare occurrence. Wyatt smiled too, because he had the raw, jangling nerves of a six-year-old who had guzzled too many energy drinks.

"Where are we?" the nurse asked.

"We're heading west up the Continental Divide, then to Glenwood Springs soon after. Once we clear the passes, we'll build speed to get through Soldier Summit in Utah."

The nurse stared him down.

Wyatt stared back. "How are—"

"None have turned," the nurse said. "Though they were stupid during the attack. All those sudden jerks didn't help any, either."

"Somebody pulled the pin," he said, "and the cars separated. We tied them together with a safety chain."

"Quick thinking."

"It was Ryle, not me. Did you see anything? Did you see who lifted the pin?"

"The train was *stopped*." The nurse's voice dripped with disappointment. "Sabotage would be easy."

Wyatt nodded. "How's—"

"No more than others," the nurse interrupted.

"Right. I just . . . " He wouldn't lose hope that his brother had the winning lottery number. Like Starla. "There was a girl we kind of rescued. She's fourteen."

The nurse frowned. "That's impossible."

Maybe not. Maybe there were scientists who could make a vaccine. Scientists, not a genius kid and a bunch of orphans. "It seems like she's immune."

"I want to see her with my own eyes," the nurse said.

"Wyatt?" Cheddar's voice came over the PA system. "The Council requests your presence in the map car. Train business."

Train business, Wyatt thought. What now. "I'm needed?" he said and kicked himself for sounding like he was asking for permission.

"Go ahead," the nurse. "But bring me the girl."

WYATT

When Wyatt entered the map car a few minutes later, Ryle was standing with Vash, Cheddar, and Tater. Diesel and Festus were also there. Diesel was stretched out on a recliner. Smiling. Not his usual smile to hide the sociopath inside, a genuine grin, full of smugness.

Diesel thought Wyatt was soft.

He thought wrong.

Vash hugged Wyatt hard and, strangely, didn't say a word, even when he dipped free of the embrace.

Cheddar cleared his throat. "While you were with the nurse, Tater and I interrogated Festus about the caboose incident. He confessed immediately."

"'Cause he was going to peel me like a tater!" Festus shrieked, pointing at Tater.

Wyatt looked at Tater, and he smirked. Festus was so gullible. Wyatt felt bad for him. "Did you lift the pin, Festus?"

Festus shook his head vehemently. "Nope. Not me."

"Did you see who did?"

Festus zipped his lips. "Diesel said Cheeseboy and Tatertot can figure it out all by their lonesome. Which of you is lonesome?"

"Could you be more stupid?" Diesel said.

Festus tilted his head, calculating the possibility. Then he said, "That was real mean, Big D."

"Lay off him, Diesel," Wyatt said. Festus was a terrible liar, and Diesel was clearly guilty. But why had he lifted the pin? "Give me one reason not to purge you."

"For what?" Diesel asked. But he hesitated, like he'd overplayed his hand. "I ain't done nothing wrong."

Wyatt shook his head at the obvious lie. "Why would you uncouple the caboose?"

"'Cause duh. Zombies were crawling all over it, and it was the easiest way to get rid of them. Right, Festus?"

Festus zipped his lips.

"Seriously? You don't have my back after I sacrifice my ear to protect you?" Diesel tried to play it off with a shrug, but the fear in his eyes betrayed him. "Whatever. I solved the problem, so why are you staring at me, Conductor?"

Wyatt tugged at his yellow wristband. "I'm deciding whether to lock you up or purge you."

"Bruh, you ain't got it in you," Diesel said. "Not after Ricky."

Wyatt froze, his body tense. Jaw set. Eyes unblinking. He waited a moment, then three, before speaking. "People we knew and cared about are on the caboose. You almost purged them."

"Nobody cares anymore," Diesel said. "The caboose's dead weight."

"Hands up." Wyatt waved the paintball gun. "Don't try to pull anything. I'd hate to shoot your eye out."

"You ain't serious," Diesel said.

"Oh, he's serious." Ryle smirked as she picked at her nails. "You should have—" Her face fell, and after a few seconds of silence, she ran toward the sleeping cars.

"Where's she going, Big D?" Festus said, scratching his head.

Diesel pointed a finger at Wyatt. "You can't keep me in a cell forever. What happens when I get out?"

"Seems simple to me," Tater said. "Throw Diesel in the caboose and let him rot."

"It's not that simple," Cheddar said. "They're hard enough to control without putting a human under their noses."

"Then dump his butt off the train," Tater said.

"That would be murder," Cheddar said.

"Not much of one." Tater laughed. "He's old. He'll turn soon anyhow."

Tater's words stung. Wyatt tried to ignore it. "Soon is soon," Wyatt said. "Soon is not now."

"Then what're we going to do with him?" Tater said. "Let him lay around in a nice clean bed eating all Cheddar's soup?"

"Soup?" Cheddar snorted. "You're standing your ground over a bowl of chicken noodle?"

"Soup's good food," Tater said. "Food keeps us alive."

"Now that I think about it, Tater's right," Wyatt said. "Diesel, it's either a cell or the caboose."

A bead of sweat popped up on Diesel's brow. "You ain't gonna give me to the nurse, little bruh. You're bluffing."

"Maybe. Maybe not." A couple of days ago, Wyatt would've admitted to bluffing. But after Marti's death, the hijacking plan, the attacks by the herds, he refused to fold. He thumbed the safety off the paintball gun. "Ever played the lottery, Diesel?"

RYLE

Three minutes after that, Ryle rushed into her sleeper compartment. She scrambled under the bed and pulled out her footlocker. She turned the tumblers on the lock then yanked, but it held fast.

"No, no, no, no! It can't be!"

She spun the dial again. This time, it clicked.

She threw the lid open and rummaged through her backpack, tossing clothes and other items aside. Then she grabbed a plain brown bag and ran to the lavatory. She locked the door twice to be sure. She pulled out a bottle of nail polish scavenged in Utah back when nail polish still mattered.

Sapphire blue.

She stared at her nails. The thumb and three of her fingers. The nails were solid black.

Get a grip. Breathe. That's it. Focus. You feel fine, and panic won't solve anything. "Here goes nothing," she said and started painting her nails.

But it wasn't nothing. It was everything.

A few minutes later, she pulled the lavatory door open and checked the room. She hid the nail polish in her footlocker, closed the lid, and fought back tears.

It seemed so abstract, turning into a zombie. When Wyatt found out, would he put her in the caboose? He said he wouldn't. But he would have to. The hunger would come, like it did with Parcheesi.

But how long did she have? Would it be over fast, as with her mom? Or would it be ever so slow, like with Wyatt's brother? Maybe she would get lucky. Maybe they would reach Nirvana before she turned, and the scientists could do a blood transfusion and give her whatever Starla had. They could save her.

"Stop it, Ryle. You don't believe in Santa Claus," she said to herself.

She grabbed the lock and snapped it shut. The snap was crisp, not the muted, worn-out tumblers she expected. The lock was red and new, not blue and scratched up from spending months on her middle school locker, the combination burned in her memory. 16-7-32.

"This isn't my . . . lock," she whispered and stared at it in disbelief.

Not the lock she had just opened. It was new. Somebody had swapped locks! She spun the dial, knowing it wouldn't work. 16-7-32. Not her combination. Not her lock. Not her secret.

"Who's there?" she said and whirled, fists up.

The door was cracked open. Nobody there. Only a crack. A crack wide enough for someone to see in.

She stuck her head outside and heard footsteps. They were light and quick and headed for the infirmary car. Festus. It had to be. That little rat was the only one sneaky enough to catch her unaware.

She locked her compartment door and made a beeline for the infirmary, expecting to see Festus. But the corridor was empty and silent except for the sound of Lucille. When she passed Starla's compartment, Ryle saw her reading a book.

"I like your nail polish," Starla mouthed.

40

RYLE

"What's the big deal?" Vash told Ryle moments later as they walked toward the sleeping compartments. "Some jerk stole your lock. Bet my boy Pez has a big old hammer we can use to smash it off."

She's not hearing me, Ryle thought, motioning for Vash to keep her voice down.

After the weird thing with Starla, Ryle had returned to her room, meaning to hide out. But her secret was weighing too heavily on her mind, and she knew she had to share it or explode. She also had to prepare Vash for what was about to happen. Somebody had to make sure the train got to Nirvana if Ryle couldn't.

"Vash, I know we can break the lock." Ryle opened her compartment door and shut it behind them when they were safe inside. "We need to find out who put it there."

"Festus would be first on my list," Vash said.

"Maybe. He was with Wyatt when I left the map car. But yeah."

"How about Diesel's boys?"

Ryle pulled out the footlocker. The new lock was shiny and bright. The face on the dial seemed to mock her. "My locker's full of all kinds of stuff. Oreos. Tools. Clothes.

Personal stuff that nobody would want."

"You got Oreos?" Vash said. "You been holding out on me?"

"Pay attention. There are bigger things happening than cookies." Ryle held out her hands. "My nails are black."

"Girl, that's blue."

"It's nail polish."

"Yes, blue nail polish. I know you know your colors."

"The polish is covering my fingernails," Ryle said, "which are turning black."

Vash gasped as the truth dawned on her. Ryle felt a flash of relief for having finally made her point, followed by a wave of regret. It squeezed her chest, made it impossible to breathe. She sucked in a tiny breath, then Vash buried her face into Ryle's neck. Her whole body shook.

Vash's tears broke something inside Ryle. The panic squeezing her chest snapped. I'm going to die, Ryle thought. But I'm not going to die for nothing. I'll get this train to Nirvana, no matter what.

"Don't you go soft on me," Ryle said. "It'll be okay."

"That's a big old lie. Diesel will fight to put you in the caboose. You know how much he hates you."

"Wyatt promised he wouldn't."

"The train won't let him keep that promise," Vash whispered. "How long do you have?"

"Cheddar says that everybody's different. It won't

happen immediately, so we've got to keep it a secret till we make it to Nirvana. It's my only hope."

"*Our* only hope," Vash said.

Ryle kicked her footlocker. Then she shook the lock. "This feels personal, Vash, like there's something else going on, and I can't see what it is. Which means I can't stand up in the next meeting and demand my lock. We'll have to out-spy the spies."

Ryle took Vash's hand. It was small and dirty, and her nails were chewed to the quicks. But the nails were still normal. From the moment they'd met in the shelter, Vash had seemed fearless. But she wasn't, was she? The chewed nails. The way she crossed herself when she didn't think anyone was looking. The worn rosary hidden under her camo jacket.

"The stories I used to read," Vash said, "about all those kids who take over 'cause the grown-ups screwed every-thing up? I always wanted to be the story's hero. The kick-butt girl with the bow and arrows, y'know? But what I wouldn't give for my nana to bring me a bowl of Blue Bell ice cream and to snuggle up to watch Netflix like a family again. 'Cause you know what, adulting sucks."

"Now we know why grown-ups sucked at it." Ryle laughed. "First thing to do is to remove the lock, so see if you can borrow a something to cut it. Bolt cutters or something."

"Pez's got tons of tools," Vash said. "But I haven't seen any bolt cutters."

Ryle pushed her locker back under her bed. Vash was right—they were on a train, not in a big box hardware store. You made do with what you had.

"Then we'll have to improvise. And then we'll investigate."

"My bet's on that little rat Festus," Vash said.

"Funny," Ryle said and smiled, "rat-hunting season just opened up."

41

DIESEL

The zombie apocalypse had been good to Diesel. It took everything away from others, but it gave him what he wanted. Until Wyatt had taken it away. Before dawn the next morning, Diesel lay in his cell, plotting revenge.

"I'll get you back, *Conductor*," he said to himself, over and over.

"Shut it! I've got a headache!"

Diesel went to the door. He looked across the corridor at the other cell. "What did you say?"

"Bad enough to get thrown in jail." A girl's face appeared in the window. "Now I've got to listen to you whine? What happened to your ear?"

"Zombie ate it. Didn't hurt that much." Diesel squinted at her. "You're the old lady."

"Yeah, the one they kidnapped."

"How old are you?"

"Fourteen."

Diesel scoffed. "Yeah right."

"I'm immune." She held up her hands. "Ten fingernails. Every one of them black."

He stared at her hands, slack-jawed. If she was immune, then they had what the scientists needed. Somebody who hadn't turned into a zombie. "They're taking you to Nirvana."

"Nirvana's a band, stupid. My dad used to listen to them."

"Duh, but it's also some super-secret project on some island." Diesel couldn't remember what songs his parents listened to. There was never music in his house. "If you're immune, you'd be pretty useful to the scientists, right? They could harvest your organs or whatever."

Starla went quiet.

"Hello?"

"Nirvana's not my style," she said after a long pause, "but I do like this train."

"Yup. Except for the loser that locked me up. The conductor. But the surprise is going to be on him pretty soon."

"What surprise?"

"I've been deer hunting. Except I've killed a lot more deer than I brought back. I stacked them by the tracks to draw the herds."

"Why would you do that?"

"Herds are full of shamblers and Dumpties. Dumpties block the tracks. The train has to slow down until the way is clear. My posse saves the day, and poof, Diesel's the conductor. I thought the plan wouldn't work until we finished the loop, but since we're following the same route back to Utah. . . . "

"Very devious. I like devious." Starla grinned. "Although deer carcasses wouldn't last even two days in the open."

"Uh, I didn't think of that."

"Of course you didn't. Anyway, how long is the loop?"

"Thousand miles, probably." Diesel smiled back at her. "But it doesn't matter. Stupid Wyatt turned the train around. Now the herds will be everywhere. Too bad I'll be locked up when they attack."

"That's a crying shame. Hey, what if I said we could make this train our own?" She winked at Diesel. "Just you and me."

"Well, sure," he said. "But we're prisoners. They might let me out, but you're going nowhere."

"I wouldn't bet my life on that."

"Not much of that left," he said, "for any of us kids."

"It wasn't the apocalypse humankind needed," she said in a singsong voice. "It was the one we deserved." She laughed. "My dad used to say that. Know what else he said? *What makes you think people are worth saving?* Crime, pollution, war, destruction? Since the grown-ups died, forests have grown, animals are everywhere, the air is clearer, and water is safe to drink. In two years. Humans had a good run, but our run is over."

"Easy for you to say. You're going to live to see it."

Starla's cell door swung open, and she unlocked Diesel's cell. "Maybe you will, too."

"Whoa," he said. "What just happened? How did you just do that?"

"Same way I've always survived—by using my wits."

"Just saying, that was a low-key flex."

"Yeah, I know. Okay, here's what we need to do—"

She gave him his orders, and he agreed. At the far end of the car, the door squeaked, and wind rushed in. Starla put a finger to her lips, then locked herself back inside. Wyatt walked straight to her cell, never even glancing at Diesel.

That's right, Diesel thought, holding his cell door closed, keep turning your back to me. See what happens.

Wyatt unlocked Starla's cell. "We're going for a walk," he said. "There's someone who wants to meet you."

42

WYATT

Wyatt led Starla to the caboose, where he knocked on the door. The viewing slot slid open. The nurse's eye was the only thing visible in the darkness of the vestibule.

"Stop wasting my time," the nurse said and closed the slot.

Wyatt reopened it. "I have a visitor. The immune girl. Open the door and see for yourself."

The slot closed.

"T-take me back," Starla said. "I-I ain't safe here."

"No one is," Wyatt said.

She scoffed, and the door swung open. They stepped into the darkness. For a breath, a sliver of light swept across the nurse's face.

The nurse grabbed Starla's wrist. "She's staying with me."

"No way," Starla said, turning toward Wyatt. "Take me back." She looked scared. Really scared.

"Shut up." The nurse produced a manacle from thin air. "And do what I tell you to."

"Stop," Wyatt said. "You wanted proof, I'm showing you proof. What're you doing?"

"Research."

"What kind of stupid research?" Starla whimpered. "If you so much as touch me, I'll make you pay. Watch and see."

The nurse didn't answer, and Wyatt let Starla's question hang in the air. He knew the answer.

"Stop fighting me," the nurse snapped.

Starla tried to break the grip on her arm. "A fight's all you're getting from me. I was playing nice, but that's gone now. Do you understand?" She looked at Wyatt. "Nice is gone!"

"Don't just stand there," the nurse said to Wyatt. "Give me a hand."

"I . . . ," Wyatt said. "I can't do this."

When Wyatt had taken Starla from the cell, he'd expected to prove to the nurse that a cure was possible. But being the conductor meant taking care of people, not letting the nurse play Dr. Frankenstein. He thought of his mom, the last time social services took him and Pike away from her. The defeated, empty look on her face. He never wanted to see that look again.

"*I* am the conductor, and this is *my* train." He pulled Starla away. "She's going back to her cell, and I won't let you experiment on her again. We'll take our chances with fairy tales."

43

CHEDDAR

An hour after Wyatt had locked Starla back in her cell, Cheddar was double-checking the corridor outside his compartment for prying eyes and Festus, which were synonymous. Seeing no one, he locked his door. He clapped twice, and the overhead lights blinked on. He pulled some textbooks down from the bookshelves. Microbiology. Pharmacology. Virology. At a corner table crammed with Petri dishes and test tubes, he gathered the notes he had taken at NPD, the drug discovery lab in Utah where, months ago, Kendra and Pike had convinced Cheddar to run experiments. Failed experiments. Dangerous experiments.

Cheddar sighed at the cramped space, the haphazard way he was forced to work. He sat down to read, then clicked on a reading lamp.

The nurse stood beside the bed. "Don't scream."

Cheddar squeaked.

The nurse wore a long coat—a duster—and a hood that hid all features. No, most features. The chin and nose Cheddar remembered protruded into the light. The duster could not mask the dank odor of rot. Or maybe the smell was embedded in the fabric. Zombie fresh didn't wash out easily.

"I need to get more serum from you."

Cheddar glanced at the table in the corner. "There's none left."

"You're lying." The nurse turned to the table and swept up the remaining tubes. They disappeared into pockets of the duster. "The formula's off or something. It's not right. You need to fix it."

Cheddar tried to swallow and could not. The experiment had been a bad idea from the start. Ricky had dreamed it up, and when Kendra heard about it at a Council meeting, it became her obsession. Cheddar and Wyatt, as guests of the Council, said that it was wrong. Ricky said Cheddar and Wyatt didn't care because they had more time to live, which had hurt Wyatt the most. In the end, they'd had to give in to the Council.

"But Wyatt—"

"I'm in charge of the caboose. I can handle Wyatt."

"Mixing blood serums is not like making soup," Cheddar said. "I cannot toss in random ingredients and season to flavor. We need the precise instruments they have at NPD. Beakers. Piping. A centrifuge. But beyond that, the odds of hitting on the correct formula using blind experimentation are no greater than winning the lottery. Ever heard of a needle in a haystack?"

"Whenever I drop a needle," the nurse said and held up a vial of blood, "I use a magnet to find it."

44

DIESEL

The cold weather had moved on, and it had gotten so warm, Diesel had ditched his coat. He sat on a dirt bike on high ground, watching the locomotive rounding the bend between Longmont and Boulder. In a few miles, Wyatt would find out that he wasn't nearly as smart as he thought he was.

"Never know what hit 'em," Diesel said to himself.

His and Starla's plan was going off without a hitch. It was his plan, really. He'd dreamed it up when Wyatt took Starla to the caboose, and she'd made a couple of changes when he brought her back. At first Diesel thought she'd want to kill more deer to leave along the track, but she'd wanted him to take the dirt bike to the ridge and deliver a message. Stealing the bike had been easy. Everybody was too distracted to notice.

Diesel lowered the binoculars, then saw something strange with his naked eye. "Antelope?"

A huge shadow was crossing the distant plains, too far away for the binoculars to pick up the details. He lowered the glasses again and glanced up at the sky. Large clouds floated toward the horizon. Shadows. The clouds were casting shadows on the ground. That explained it. His eyes were playing tricks on him.

"Hands up," a voice behind him said. "Don't make a sound, just like before."

Before? His mind raced. The store in Cheyenne, where he'd heard this voice the first time.

"What's Starla's message?" the voice said.

"She says . . . " He wracked his brains to say it exactly. Get it right, she had warned him. Your life depends on it. "She says, look for the bull with the purple eye."

"Purple eye? That's it?"

He remembered it distinctly now. "Yes, that's it. Look for the bull with the purple eye."

"Take these with you," the feral said and handed him a box of spearguns. "Wait five minutes, then leave. When you get to the train, go to the helipad and wave your shirt like a flag. Keep waving until we signal you to stop."

Diesel frowned. "What's the signal?"

"You'll know."

"How?"

Diesel waited several minutes for a response, but none came. Slowly he turned his head. Nobody there, like he'd been visited by a ghost.

Diesel checked his watch. Time to catch the train, which was a few miles ahead now, snaking toward Boulder. He tucked the binoculars inside his jacket and gunned the accelerator. The rear tire threw rocky dirt in a rooster tail that he looked back to admire before the bike rocketed down the arroyo.

At the bottom of the ridge, the path widened, and a skein of hard-packed earth ran alongside the tracks. He waved at the flatcar. For a few seconds, nothing happened, then Festus appeared at the top of the ramp and waved back.

"Drop the ramp!" Diesel yelled.

Festus pulled the heavy security bolt that held the ramp into place, and seconds later the ramp pivoted on its hinge and dropped beside the train.

Diesel gunned it and drove the bike straight onto the flatcar. "Woo-hoo!" he said. "Did you see that?"

"Yup," said Ryle, leveling the bō at him. "I saw it, and now Wyatt is going to hear about it. Start walking."

45

RYLE

After the locker incident, Ryle had decided to keep tabs on Festus by following him and learning his routines. His actions seemed pretty random, except when he ran errands for Diesel. When she saw him sneak off after dinner, she suspected he was up to no good. Those suspicions were confirmed when she found Diesel's empty cell.

"Where did he go?" she had asked Starla, who was staring out her own cell door.

"You people are the real monsters," Starla had muttered, then her voice was drowned out by the roar of a dirt bike.

"Hold that thought," Ryle had said and rushed to the flatcar.

It was evening, and the warm weather was turning cold again. The train was nearing Louisville when she'd spotted Festus lowering the ramp, then Diesel driving up it.

"You can't stop me," Diesel whined as Ryle marched him through the cars. "I'll escape again."

"I can, and I did."

"On whose authority?"

"The conductor's."

"I was doing the right thing." Diesel turned to defend himself. "Wyatt's too weak to conduct. Help us, and I'll make sure you reach Nirvana."

"Shut up and move," Ryle said and pushed him ahead, which was a mistake.

Diesel was faster than he looked. As she pushed, he spun and grabbed her bō. Before Ryle could react, he punched her jaw and slammed her into a seat.

"Ow!" Ryle struggled to her feet as Diesel took off. "Come back here, jerk!"

He ran to the boxcar ahead, then climbed its side ladder to the roof. Ryle took a couple of stumbling steps, but quickly found her balance. She followed him to the top of the boxcar and saw both Diesel and Festus reach the helipad. Diesel pulled off his shirt and was waving it over his head. Festus did the same thing.

"He's signaling someone," she said and started running.

When she reached the helipad, Festus took off, but Diesel kept at it. His pale skin had turned raw and red.

"Stop!" Ryle yelled. "You've got no idea what you're doing!"

"Make me!" Diesel yelled back.

"You're playing with fire! Parcheesi did that once, and she wasn't happy with what showed up!"

"You won't be, either!"

"Where'd Festus go?" she shouted. It wasn't like him to leave Diesel's side.

"Right here!"

Ryle turned around. Wyatt was near the edge of the helipad, holding Festus by the collar. Vash was scrambling up onto the roof behind him.

"Vash saw Diesel on the dirt bike!" Wyatt yelled. "Your stunt is finished, Diesel!"

"Wanna bet?" Diesel yelled and pointed east. The plains were filled with Dumpties, shamblers, and zombie fresh, all mixed together. "Now you're going to pay!"

"Holy zombie land!" Vash said. "Why are there so many?"

Wyatt pointed out the roadkill that dotted the railbed. "Look down!"

There were dozens of deer carcasses along the tracks, partially hidden by tall prairie grass. Some of them were picked down to the bone, but most were surrounded by packs of zombie fresh, who were fighting each other for the meat.

Bait.

Bait to draw zombies to the tracks. The thought made Ryle shudder. It was a trap. "Somebody's been feeding them," she yelled.

"Like who?" Vash called back.

"Somebody who wants to stop the train." Wyatt pointed at Diesel. "Drop the shirt, Big D. You're done."

Ryle heard Diesel laugh right before something pinched her belly. Her body jerked, and her hands flew out to the side. She went rigid, and the pinching pain became a steel bear trap slamming closed on her gut. She looked down and saw the red fletching of the arrow that had impaled her. *That'll leave a great scar.* Then she felt nothing, and her legs gave out.

"Ryle!" Vash screamed.

Ryle was looking at the sky, and Wyatt's face came into view. She looked down as the pool of blood on her shirt grew larger.

"Are you okay?" Wyatt asked.

Vash pushed a palm against her forehead. "She's been shot! Of course she's not okay!"

"She's going into shock," Wyatt said. "Festus, give me your shirt!"

Festus hesitated, but Wyatt ripped it from his hand. He folded the shirt until it was a hard pack of cloth. "We need pressure. This is going to hurt. A lot."

He jammed the shirt inside Ryle's waistband. She screamed and her head rolled forward.

"Ryle? Ryle!" Vash's eyes widened. She covered her mouth. "My girl is going to be all right, Wyatt? Right?"

Ryle wanted to answer, to reassure her friend that it was all good, but when she tried to speak, no words came. Everything went silent before everything went black.

46

RYLE

Ryle's mom used to say that the world was your oyster, and you could have your pick of pearls. Except Ryle didn't want to pick. She wanted it all. Dancing, art, music, grades, scholarships, friends, basketball trophies, medals. A whole string of pearls.

After the zombies came, they were told to evacuate to an emergency shelter. "Soldiers will save us," Ryle's mom had said as they had boarded a school bus at Clarkson and Belleview.

The bus was one of dozens the Colorado National Guard had commandeered to transport survivors to Denver's Green Zone. The zone was sterile, they said, free of zombies and protected by armed guards.

"Soldiers will save us," her mom had repeated as she steered Ryle to the back of the bus. "But if there's trouble, we'll be close to the emergency exit. We've got to take care of our own."

Her mom took the aisle, and Ryle took the window seat, which trapped her against the side of the bus. Other passengers got on. Moms with kids. Kids with kids. Kids by themselves. Ryle watched them warily, with a hand on her grandma's bō. Her mom and the bō,

Ryle had them both. Her mom to protect her, and the staff to protect her mom.

After the last passenger boarded, the doors closed and the bus took off.

"They're in a hurry," her mom said and coughed. Her voice was raspy and harsh. She popped a cough drop into her mouth and patted Ryle's knee, though they both knew Ryle was too old for knee pats. "Allergies are acting up."

The bus rumbled down Belleview then onto Broadway. Out the window, the world looked normal, except for the thin layer of ash coating everything. Ryle closed her eyes and dozed off.

A scream woke her, and when she opened her eyes, the bus was dark, and there was so much growling.

"Mom?" Ryle called.

The others were running down the center aisle, knocking each other down to escape the moving bus. But there was one kid left behind. A tiny girl in a yellow dress and sneakers. She was sucking her thumb, too terrified to move, and Ryle's mom was lunging for her with hands curled like claws.

"Mom! No!" Ryle screamed.

She vaulted the seat and grabbed the little girl and practically threw her into the arms of another woman. Then she turned and snatched her mom's hands and tried to stop her. But her mom was too strong, and Ryle was too small.

Her mother threw her aside, then growled, blood dripping from her mouth.

"No!" Ryle screamed and in a panic, grabbed her bō and backpack and hit the emergency exit.

Then she was falling to the pavement and running down the dark streets, away from the bus, away from the monster her mom had just become, and back toward the city, where the skies were bright with fire. After two days of running, she'd collapsed from exhaustion. She'd awakened in a shelter, stretched out on a dirty cot in a room without windows. There were kids crying, the low, sad cries of kids in such pain, all they could do was moan.

"You can get up now," a girl had said somewhere in the darkness. "I know you're awake."

Ryle hadn't wanted to open her eyes and find someone other than her mom beside her. "How'd you know I was awake?"

"'Cause you snore like a chainsaw," the girl said. "Let's go get food. You've got to be starving."

"I'm not hungry," Ryle said, although she was, but the thought of eating made her stomach turn.

Ryle sat up. The girl was staring at her. She was skinny with curly hair, glasses, and a pair of too-big Doc Marten boots. There was a backpack on the cot beside her and a coloring book on her lap.

"Where did you get the crayons?" Ryle said.

"Crayolas," the girl said. "Sixty-four colors and I use 'em all." She stuffed the box of crayons and the coloring book into the backpack. She slung the pack over her shoulder. "Come on, let's go before the other kids eat the Oreos and we get stuck with broccoli and kale."

"What's wrong with kale?" Ryle asked.

"It's bitter," the girl said and grinned. "Like you."

"You're salty. I like salty," Ryle had said. "What's your name?"

"I used to be somebody named Vashandra. Now I'm Vash, and you're my family. What's your name?"

Ryle had almost said her name, then realized she used to be somebody else, too. "Call me Ryle."

When Ryle awoke a couple hours later in the infirmary, Wyatt sat beside her bed. His eyes were closed. His breathing was steady and deep, and out the window, she saw snow blowing across the night sky. She sucked in, anticipating sharp pains, but there was not much more than a sting, and she realized that it was the tape on the bandages tugging on her skin.

"How do you feel?" he said.

She jumped at his voice. "I'm okay. Thought you were asleep."

"Resting my eyes." He yawned. "It's been a long day."

"You were watching me the whole time? Creeper."

"Keeping an eye on you while Vash got dinner. Other than that, mostly thinking."

"Where are we?" she asked.

"Berkley. A couple hours south of Louisville."

"Isn't that where Marti got shot?"

He nodded. "Some coincidence, huh?"

"Yeah." She shrugged. "Do you ever miss your parents?"

"That came from nowhere," he said. "Never heard you mention grown-ups before."

That was true. Vash never mentioned hers, either. Ryle's dad had never been in the picture, but her mom was always in her thoughts. "So, do you?"

"My life went off the rails early," he said and returned her shrug. "My parents split when I was two. My mom waited tables for a couple years. Then she got sick, and the state stuck me and my brother in foster care and left her to look after herself. Which she couldn't do."

"I'm sorry."

"She died when I was seven." His voice was harsh and gritty. "My foster family took me to the funeral, but Pike's family wouldn't go. So he bolted. After that, no foster home could hold him, and he ended up in a group house a hundred miles away. It took a zombie apocalypse for us to find each other again."

He stared at the floor. Ryle wondered how a person could be right next to you and still feel so distant. She stared at her blue fingernails and tried not to imagine the black bubbling through the polish.

"There's something I need to tell you," she said. He was going to find out, and it was better if it came from her.

"First I've got news of my own." He smiled at her. "I've been thinking a lot and I decided that when we reach Salt Lake, we're all going with you. The whole train. We're staying on Lucille and heading straight to Nirvana."

"Nirvana or bust," Ryle said and her chest tingled with a feeling of hope so rare she wanted more than anything to hang on to it forever.

47

STARLA

Later that night, Starla was sleeping when a hand covered her mouth. That stink. She recognized it. It smelled like Lich, and for half a second, she thought he was in the room. Then in the dim light, she saw the hood and knew who the intruder was.

"You," she rasped.

"Quiet," the nurse said. "All I want is a little more blood."

Starla tried to fight, but the nurse was strong, maybe stronger than Lich. Starla smelled a strong chemical odor, and the fight went from her.

Starla wasn't big or strong, but she had brains and instincts. She'd always been sneaky enough to do anything she wanted, then smile her way out of trouble, but it sucked being the oldest girl in the world. Then one day she saw Lich standing on a manhole cover. His clothes were dirty, he had rope burns on his arms, and his eyes were black as ink. He didn't immediately try to chew her face off, so she instinctively raised her hand to wave, and he waved back.

"Are you dead?" she asked.

"Noff," he said.

The word wasn't that clear. It was more like a sound. But it was definitely a no.

"My name's Starla," she said. "What's yours?"

"Lich," he said, like he was trying to swallow the letters.

"Lich," she said. "You're a zombie, but you can talk."

He nodded, and his jaws clacked.

"That makes you special. Very special."

"Spushal." A single black blood tear rolled down his face. "Sumbie."

She was standing there, trying to digest all of this, when another zombie loped around the corner. This one was fast. It was hungry. It came right for her, moving blindingly fast, arms out, bloodlust on its face.

I'm what's for dinner, Starla thought.

"Stopt!" Lich commanded, and the just-turned zombie stopped. "Goh!" Lich said, and it loped away.

"Lich," Starla had said, grinning, "how'd you like to help me rule the world?"

Starla called Lich her boyfriend because she liked the sound of it. Boyfriend sounded better than a trained attack dog. Then one day, she and Lich had been patrolling down by the railroad tracks when they heard a long whistle. Starla followed the sound. There was a train rolling through the rail yard. A freaking train. What were the odds?

Lich started growling and keening. As the train passed by, he lifted his arm and pointed. "Hum," he said.

She wasn't sure what he meant at first. But then he said it again and again and again. Hum, hum, hum.

Home.

"Were you on that train?" she asked.

He nodded, jaw clacking. "Kilt me. Mud me gurbige." Garbage.

"But you're not dead?" she said. "What do you mean they killed you and made you garbage?"

He held up his arms. His wrists were covered with pock marks. He stuck out a foot, and his ankle had the same marks.

"Gurbage," he said, making it very clear.

"Oh," she said. "They threw you off because you were turning into a zombie?"

He clacked again. "Spurmits."

Before, she might have felt sympathy. That's what other people felt in moments like this. Their hearts would break, and they'd comfort him. She didn't feel any of that, of course. But she could use his sadness, his weakness. Weaponize it.

A train would be a lovely thing to have, she thought, watching it disappear between row after row of rusting freight cars. "You know what, Lich? Zombies need love, too." She patted his shoulder, almost tenderly. "The mean people need to pay."

"Payths."

"That's right, they need to pay, and you and I are going to make them."

He shook his head. "C'nt stoth trun." Can't stop the train.

"Oh, sweetie," Starla said, "I bet we can."

48

WYATT

Heavy snow was falling when the train reached Denver the next morning. Right back where we started, Wyatt thought, then said over the PA, "Riders aged ten and over report to the first coach car."

He sat down to wait, eyes closed, hands clasped together, rehearsing what he was going to say. His stomach was suddenly full of butterflies, and he felt the paralyzing weight of looming failure on his shoulders. So many things he didn't know. Like why did the parasite only attack adults? What had happened to other kids in other cities? Were there more hiding out there? Did they stick together like the riders of the zombie train, or had they turned on one another? Was that the kind of kid who had shot Ryle? Was it the same shooter who had killed Marti? Who was Diesel signaling? Diesel had looked so shocked when Ryle was shot, he hadn't even tried to defend himself.

Within five minutes, the coach was full. Ryle and Vash were the last to arrive, and Wyatt was surprised to see them. Ryle was propped up by Vash, who was acting like a human crutch. Cheddar had removed the bolt quickly, used lidocaine to numb the pain, and had bandaged the wound, muttering about the dangers of infection. Ryle would be sore later, he'd warned. She looked more sour than sore now.

Wyatt shook his hands to get the nervousness out. "Thanks for coming together," he said. "I know a lot's been happening, and you have questions."

With all eyes on him, he explained about the zombie attacks, about Starla, and to the anger of many, about Diesel's betrayal. It settled Wyatt's mind to put things in order. His voice grew stronger.

"When we make Utah, Lucille is not turning back." He held up a hand to quiet them. "The loop has been like home, and nobody likes to leave a good home. But the loop isn't home. Lucille is, and we're going to stick together."

"Why now?" Tater said. "Why can't we wait to see what happens?"

"Wish we could," Wyatt said. "But Ryle, Cheddar, and me are all getting older. Pez and Diesel are pretty close to our age, too. If we wait too long, it'll be too late for everybody."

Tater crossed his arms. "You're saying that so we'll agree."

"Wyatt is right," Ryle said, looking at Wyatt. "I've got the . . . I'm going to . . . It's inevitable."

Wyatt remembered the scars on her body. He knew she'd planned to betray them with Parcheesi. He knew that she was hiding a secret. He knew that he shouldn't trust her. But he did.

"If she's gonna turn," Tater said, "she gets locked up. Just like my sister."

"Tater," Vash said, rising, "you better watch that mouth."

"Stick to the subject." Wyatt stepped between them. "Cheddar, go get Pez. My plan depends on him, so he has to buy into it. He'll say he can't come, that Lucille's boiler is overheating, or the control box is fritzing, so threaten him."

Cheddar looked disappointed but agreed. "Please don't make any rash decisions while I'm gone."

"Tater," Ryle said after Cheddar had departed. "You're right. Wyatt, it's time for me to—"

"No." Wyatt helped her to her feet. They stood shoulder to shoulder. He wanted to show a united front. "You've got time."

"But the rules," Ryle said.

Wyatt nodded slowly. Yes. The rules. Nobody's bigger than the train. Never stop the train. Everybody ends up in the caboose. The rules had kept them alive. But the rules meant they had no future.

"Rules were meant to protect us, not hurt us," he said. "Every single rider matters more than this train."

FESTUS

From his hiding spot in a dark corner of the engine room, Festus was spying on the engineer. Pez was in the cab, telling Lucille that she'd handled bigger snows than this. Spying on Pez was boring. He never left Lucille except to use the latrine or catnap. It wasn't naptime yet, so Festus was waiting for Pez to need to go. He had been waiting a long time, and Festus needed to go real bad himself. But Big D had warned him not to leave, and he didn't want to disappoint his best friend again. He was looking around for a can or something when he heard heavy footsteps clanging on the locomotive deck.

Cheeseboy.

Quiet as a mouse, Festus nibbled his fingers and watched Cheddar stomp past, kicking snow off his boots, then tap Pez on the shoulder.

When Pez turned, his smile fell. "Thought you'd be Vash."

"Wyatt wants you," Cheddar shouted.

"Huh?" Pez cupped a hand to his ear, pretending not to hear. "Dogs won, too?"

"I said," Cheddar shouted again, his voice cracking. "Wyatt wants you in the map car for a meeting."

Festus giggled and slapped a hand over his mouth. This was way better than a pee break. Pez would leave. He did everything the conductor told him to. Big D was so smart. He knew Cheeseboy would come. Maybe Big D even tricked Cheeseboy into coming.

"What?" Pez shouted. "I can't leave Lucille. We've just turned for Arvada, and it's real tight going through that town."

Cheddar pulled out a Snickers bar. "Wyatt said to bring you by any means necessary!"

Pez snatched the candy bar and pressed a button on the control board. "Watch Lucille for me, Ched. Got to be back in five minutes, tops. Once we hit the Leyden, it's gonna get even more hairy."

Festus shrunk into the corner as Pez thumped past and Cheddar followed for a few feet to make sure the engineer left. Woo-hoo! Time make Big D proud!

He snuck into the cabin and dropped into the engineer's seat, giggling. His fingertips tingled. They always did when he was doing something bad. Like stealing Vienna sausages. Or playing the spy game for Big D. They got especially itchy when he got sent on a secret mission—like this one.

He rolled up his sleeve and he reviewed the instructions written on his arm. They were simple and numbered.

1. Push the button.

2. Turn this knob.

3. Pull that handle.

"In that order," Big D had said.

He searched for a button and a knob but only found a doohickey and a thingamabob. He shrugged, oh well, and pushed a couple of blinking red lights, then pulled a long lever. Something popped, and there was a big clunk.

"Hey!" Cheddar shouted from the corridor. "Don't touch that!"

There was a soft boom inside the engine. Then an ear-splitting whine. An acid smell rose from the engine compartment, and the cab filled with smoke so thick, it blocked out all light. But Festus felt like a kid who'd won a carnival prize. "Woo-hoo!" he crowed and was still giggling when an angry explosion blew him out of his shoes.

50

RYLE

"What's so important that I had to leave Lucille?" Pez said as he stomped into the map car. "There's a foot of snow and—"

BOOM!

A blast swept down the train, and everyone hit the floor. The map car rocked back and forth, violently bucking. Thick, black smoke billowed past the coach windows.

"Lucille!" Pez screamed and took off running, with Vash right behind him.

"Fire drill!" Wyatt yelled, pointing at Tater. "Lock down the littles!"

Tater scrambled for the PA mic, and his voice was echoing through the train as Ryle painfully followed Wyatt from the car and struggled up the ladder to the top. There, Ryle stopped, bent over with pain, and was lost in a cloud of roiling smoke.

"Oh, no," she said.

Wyatt, Vash, and Pez ran ahead, and Ryle followed slowly. When she reached the fuel car, she heard Vash yelling, "Fire! Engine one is on fire!"

Then she heard Wyatt scream, "Pez! Stop!" as she jumped from the fuel car to the locomotive. Pain shot through her guts, and she went down to one knee.

"Lucille!" Pez cried. He flung the cab door open and plunged into the shroud of roiling smoke.

Vash tried to follow but fell back, waving the thick fumes away. "He's gonna get himself killed," she yelled, coughing violently.

"Stay here!" Wyatt told Ryle and Vash. He covered his mouth with his T-shirt and disappeared into the smoke.

Ryle struggled to her feet, then pulled Vash into a hug. She prayed that Wyatt wasn't being stupid, that he knew the engine room like the back of his hand. Rushing into the locomotive was a dumb thing to do, but brave, too.

A moment passed.

Then another.

"What's taking so long?" Vash asked.

"Give them a chance," Ryle said as much to herself as to Vash.

Surely they could make it through a little smoke. Then the other side of her brain—the one that had hit the emergency exit and abandoned her mom so long ago—told her to run. Like her mom always said, you've got to take care of your own. She should take Vash and the littles and run.

No. No. Not again. There would be no more emergency exits.

Black smoke billowed from the engineer's window, the brakeman's window, through the ventilation vents, up through the spaces in the decking, between the wheels, and from the drive shaft. Lucille was seeping smoke from every pore.

"Wyatt!" Ryle yelled. "Hurry your butt up!"

Another moment passed, and Vash's shoulders began to shake. Ryle wanted to comfort her. There was nothing left to say, only worry and fear and what if, what if, what if.

Then the smoke parted, and Wyatt burst from the engine room, dragging Pez by the strap of his overalls.

"Pez!" Vash shouted.

"Wyatt," Ryle said and relief whispered through her.

Wyatt handed Pez off to Vash and fell to his hands and knees, coughing.

"Let me go!" Pez screamed and tried to get up. "I'll kill him!"

Ryle planted a boot on his chest. "Stay down!"

He fought to get up but was too weak, and his breath wouldn't come. "Lucille," he cried.

"Can be repaired!" Wyatt shouted. "Who do you want to kill?"

"Festus," Pez wheezed. "The rat-faced dingus hurt Lucille!"

Ryle lurched to her feet and ran for the cab. "Is Festus still in there?"

"Ryle!" Vash and Wyatt both screamed.

Ryle held her breath, but her eyes were squirting water,

and she couldn't see a thing. Her hands went out instinctively. Scorched air touched her fingers. She yelped and drew back like she'd touched a hot stove.

"Festus!" She turned, then turned again. "Where are you? Say something!"

Where is he? she thought. Think, Ryle. Where would he be? Floor. On the floor. Get low. Don't breathe. Poisoned air filled her lungs as she crawled forward. Her hands found an arm. She felt hair and a pointy chin. Then she touched a face and felt something warm and sticky.

"Didn't mean to hurt Lucille," Festus whispered. "Big D said it'd help."

She was terrified and wanted to shake him. "Help what? Festus! What did Diesel tell you to do? Tell me!"

Her angry yelling used up her breath, and when she inhaled, the thick smoke felt like it was chewing through her lungs. It was impossible to see, to hear, to breathe.

"Zombies," Festus wheezed, "are our friends."

Then hands were on her shoulders, and Wyatt pulled her back. "Out!" he shouted, pushing her in the direction of the door.

Ryle stumbled blindly toward the glow of daylight. Seconds later she was out and collapsing into Vash's arms.

"I got you," Vash said, helping her down to the deck. "Breathe, girl, keep breathing."

"Can't," she whispered. "Hurts too much."

Vash smacked her on the back. "I said breathe!"

Ryle sucked in fresh air. Coughs wracked her body. Her ears rang, and her head was about to explode, then she felt her body relax, and when she opened her bleary eyes, Wyatt was dragging someone out by the arms. He leaned over the body, giving CPR.

"Oh, no," Vash said, putting both hands over her eyes. "Poor kid."

Ryle blinked hard, trying to clear her eyes. She heard a sharp cough to her left, where Festus lay on his side, taking ragged breaths. Whew. What a relief. But if Festus was beside her, who had Wyatt just dragged out?

51

WYATT

The train had stopped. It was two hours past sunset, and a heavy snow was falling, and the train had stopped. The one unbreakable rule had been broken, and Wyatt did not care. He lowered Cheddar's still body to the examination table in the infirmary. The same table where Cheddar had patched up every rider at some point. Wyatt himself had been stitched together four times, and none of that had hurt as much as seeing his best friend lying so still.

"He's heavy," Ginny said. "How did you carry him by yourself?"

"He didn't feel heavy."

A rush of adrenaline hadn't given Wyatt superhuman strength. There hadn't been a rush at all, even when he had given Cheddar CPR, until Vash had broken into tears, and Ryle had pulled him away. He was the conductor. It was his job to fix this. He held his rage inside, where it built like steam trapped inside a white-hot boiler. He'd started CPR immediately, using what he'd learned from the Red Cross class in PE, compressing Cheddar's chest to the beat of the BeeGee's "Stayin' Alive." Sweat had poured from his forehead, and his shoulders ached, and his hands were killing him, and still Cheddar hadn't been breathing.

"What happened?" Ginny asked. She pulled a sheet from a metal cabinet, trying not to look at the body. "I mean, what caused it."

"Engine malfunction. He was babysitting Lucille for Pez so I could talk to Pez about—" About hope and possibilities, taking a chance on life and being able to live. All the things that Nirvana stood for. "Something went sideways."

"Sideways?"

"Yeah." He realized that the why didn't matter. More information would only lead to more questions. Questions he couldn't answer. How are you going to fix this? he asked himself.

Ginny tucked the sheet under Cheddar's chin. "Well, whatever caused it, I'm glad you were there."

After an eternity had passed and Cheddar still hadn't moved, Wyatt had almost given up. Then, with a gasp, Cheddar took a breath, then another. Then rolled onto his side and coughed out smoke-stained mucus. Wyatt fell beside him, exhausted, and almost wept with relief.

"He's unconscious, I think," Ginny said. "But I don't really know how to treat him."

Wyatt nodded. Cheddar had been training Ginny for the last couple of months. She was good at cuts and bumps, but she wasn't ready for this. "Let's watch him and make sure he's breathing okay."

Ginny nodded and put a hand over her mouth. She was about to lose it.

"I've got this," he whispered, and put an arm around her. "Go find Tater. Tell him I said you need some milk and Oreos."

"Tater's mean," she said, "and I don't need an Oreo."

"Then go help with Festus."

"But he's the one who caused this."

"He's still a rider, and we take care of our own."

She nodded and ran from the infirmary. Who could blame her? Wyatt wanted to run, too.

He clenched his jaw and tried to make his hands stop shaking, but he couldn't force the fear away. What would they do without Cheddar? He was their walking Swiss Army knife. He closed his eyes and pictured a quiet place—a still mountain lake with a solitary weeping willow—and that worked for a minute or so. But when he opened his eyes, the anxiety congealed in his chest again. It felt like an infection that he couldn't shake. Diesel. The thing that was forever caught in his chest was Diesel. He wanted Diesel to suffer the gut-wrenching pain that was eating away his own insides.

Stop it, he told himself. You had one job, and you didn't get it done. That's on you. You're the conductor. Don't get stuck on Diesel. Think about Cheddar.

If they'd been comic book characters, Cheddar would

be the faithful sidekick. Except Wyatt was nobody's superhero. He had celebrated his twelfth birthday two weeks ago. Celebrated by trying to pretend it never happened. Three hundred days ago, he'd been just another overachieving ward of the state, training for Science Olympiad with his best friends, Cheddar and Tuna. Their team had taken a gold medal at regionals, and their teacher was sure with Cheddar's scientific knowledge, Tuna's superhuman recall of trivia, and Wyatt's leadership and strategy, they could win states. Now he was the oldest boy on the planet, and it sucked more than a black hole.

Wyatt remembered what Cheddar had told him, over and over again. You're more than your brother's shadow. Wyatt wouldn't focus on getting revenge on Diesel for Cheddar's injuries but on honoring his wishes. He would keep the train rolling for his one and only best friend.

They would make it to Nirvana.

52

RYLE

The next morning, as the snow continued to swirl outside the windows of the infirmary car, Ryle sat beside Festus. He lay unconscious, bandaged head to toe, his face masked with burn cream. It had been a long night for the poor kid, but as the sun rose, he seemed to be doing better.

Couldn't say the same for Lucille. The train was stopped, and Vash and Pez were working feverishly to get the engine going. They were a sitting duck, and Wyatt had spent the night manically pacing the cars, checking the engine, checking the littles, checking the patients. Like he was walking the razor edge of panic.

"BP is 110 over 72," Ginny said. "Pulse 78. The books say it's normal for a nine-year-old."

"He's just nine?" Ryle said. "I thought he was way older." Now she despised Diesel even more. All the kid ever wanted was a friend, and Diesel took advantage of that.

Ryle dutifully wrote down the data. Ginny insisted on it, even though Ryle saw no point. Who were they keeping the records for if Cheddar wasn't there to file them?

Cheddar. How were they going to reach Nirvana without him? She'd seen kids injured before. Why did it bother her so much this time? She had to fight the urge to flee in panic, not just the infirmary car, but the whole train. But she couldn't. She had made a promise to protect her kids.

Wyatt burst through the carriage door, looking like a simmering volcano. He had scratches on his face and burns on his hands, and there was a shiner darkening his eye. "How's Ched?"

Ginny filled him in. Cheddar was stable but still unconscious, and she wasn't sure what was wrong with him. It seemed like the whole train wanted to watch over him, and Ginny had to keep shooing them out.

"That's good, that's good," Wyatt said ,and nodded robotically, like the news wasn't sinking in. "And how's Festus?"

"He's alive," Ginny said and crossed her arms. "No thanks to his *best friend*."

As for Ryle? She wanted somebody's head. She looked at Wyatt. "Diesel is going to get us all killed."

"Diesel's locked up," Wyatt said, an edge in his voice. "How's Festus? Can he talk? I have questions."

"Festus can't answer any questions when he's unconscious." Ryle snapped a chemical cold compress and handed it to Wyatt. "He's lucky to be alive."

"What's this?" Wyatt said.

"Cold compress. For your face." Ryle watched him frown. It was like he didn't know the bruises were there. "Pez did a number on it."

He tried to hand it to Ginny. "Save it for somebody who needs it."

"It's frozen now, and there's no way to use it again." Ginny pushed it back at him. "Waste not."

"Want not." He held the compress against his face. Then winced and sucked air through his teeth. "Dang, that hurts."

"Bruises usually do," Ryle said, sounding more like a smart aleck than she'd intended. She wanted to show him sympathy, but she had forgotten how.

"Is he asleep or knocked out?"

"Medicated," Ginny said. "That's what the books said to do, since we used up all the burn cream."

"Try Aquaphor for the burns." Wyatt put down the ice pack. "My mom used to work in restaurants. When she got burned, they'd slather Aquaphor all over and wrap it up airtight."

"It might work," Ryle said to Ginny, who began checking the stock. She turned to Wyatt. "Thought you said that your mom wasn't a waitress?"

Wyatt shook his head. "Line cook. Could grab a red-hot skillet with her bare hands. They were covered in scars. She used to come home in the morning after working all night and smoke a cigarette on the back porch. That scarred her lungs so bad, she died from it."

"Aquaphor for burns," Ginny said, thinking out loud.

"Wonder why Cheddar never told me that?"

"Because even a Swiss Army knife can't think of every-thing." Wyatt sat down heavily. "Ginny, take a break. Ryle and I'll watch him."

Ginny saw the look on Wyatt's face and silently trun-dled from the infirmary.

"Answer my question," Ryle said. "What are you going to do with him?"

"Festus?"

"Diesel."

"We chained him to a footlocker. It'll do till we decide what to do with him."

"When will that be?"

"It depends on what Festus says when he wakes up. Because Diesel denies everything."

"You believe that?" she snorted.

"He almost killed my best friend, so no, I don't."

Ryle held her tongue because she could see the pain on his face. But Wyatt seemed a little out of it, and he was moving too cautiously. If it had been Vash hurt, a purge would be the best thing Diesel could expect.

"But Diesel stays aboard till we figure out why Festus sabotaged the train," Wyatt said. "In the meantime, the sun is rising. That means Pez and Vash have got only a cou-ple hours to repair Lucille's engine before we've got the Big Ten Curve to deal with. If we don't build up speed going into the Continental Divide, Lucille will never make it."

"A couple hours? That's it?"

"We're between a rock and a hard place," Wyatt said. "If we stay here, the herd will swarm us. But if we can't build speed, we won't make the Big Ten Curve. We usually came down the curves, not up them. The curves were designed to slow trains down for the eastward descent. If we hit it wrong, Lucille will massively derail."

"Wyatt?"

"Yeah?" he said and tilted his head, curious.

"Are you going to put me in the caboose?"

"I already said no. Why are you asking again?"

"Because I'm not stupid." *Say it.* "Because it's where you put kids when they start to turn. Even brothers."

He paused to let the word brother hang in the air. "How'd you figure it out?"

"Seriously, never try your hand at poker. You've got the worst tells ever."

Wyatt looked out the window like he could find an answer in the blowing snow. "Yeah, Pike's back there."

"Has he turned?"

"Not completely. Sometimes, it happens fast." He snapped his fingers. "Other times, it takes a long time."

"Is that why you agreed to go to Nirvana? To save him?"

He shook his head. "Cheddar says that it's too late for Pike. He thinks that once kids start turning, they never come back. Kind of like putting an omelet back into an egg."

"Starla did," she said.

"Cheddar thinks the parasite never crossed her blood-brain barrier," he said. "Or maybe she's got chemicals in her brain that keep the parasite from growing. It'll take somebody a whole lot smarter than us to figure it out. If there's anybody smarter still alive."

Bang! There was a loud backfire, then a massive squeal, and the train lurched forward. Then it started rolling.

Ryle caught her balance then pumped a fist. "Yes!"

The PA crackled. "We're back underway, zombie train!" Vash called. "How's that for service?"

Relief flooded Wyatt's face, then he looked embarrassed. "Guess it didn't take Pez and Vash hours after all."

"You know," Ryle said, "Marti thought that having feelings makes you weak, and that leaders can't be weak. But that's a lie. Having feelings makes you human, and now more than ever, a human is what this train needs."

"Thanks," he said, standing and walking to the window. "Son of a biscuit eater! Can we not catch a freaking break?"

Ryle whipped her head around. "What?"

"Stay here! Guard Ched and Festus!"

He slammed the door open and ran toward the sleeper cars. Seconds later there was a rolling, booming noise in the distance. It was so loud that it shook the windows.

"Was that thunder?" Ryle said and leaned over to look out the windows, expecting to see storm clouds in the sky.

But the noise wasn't thunder. It wasn't thunder at all, and any hope she had felt seeped from her like water swirling down a drain.

"Stampede," she whispered.

53

WYATT

From the top of the map car, Wyatt could see all the way from Arvada, a suburb west of Denver, to the skyscrapers downtown. In between there were thousands of deserted buildings, roads littered with garbage, and countless abandoned cars. He could see the sky dumping buckets of snow across the valley. And he could also see more zombies than he'd even dreamed existed pushing through the snow-covered ruins like a slow-moving flood.

The land was low and flat here, the prairie grass taller than the snowfall. The wind was gusting, and the grass was moving back and forth, and there was a low noise like a murmur coming from all around.

Ryle stood beside him. "Oh, wow," she said. "That's kind of terrifying. I'm glad the train is moving."

Even through snowdrifts, the zombies were closing in by the second. It was like Wyatt and Ryle were neck-deep in a frozen nightmare as the rising sun fought through the mist that cloaked the herd. Their jaws hung open. Bloodred eyes bulged with hunger. Mouths pocked with rotting teeth, jaws gaping wide, groaning, and clicking.

"This is what Diesel meant," Wyatt said, "when he said we walked straight into their trap."

"What're you talking about?" Ryle asked. "Somebody put this herd of zombies in front of us? How is that possible?"

Wyatt had gotten it wrong from the beginning. The herd they met in Cheyenne had not suddenly been there. The zombies were all part of the same massive, organized swarm, and they were descending upon the train, as surely as if they were rats coming after a baited trap. He hadn't seen the big picture, and neither had Cheddar. His breath caught at the thought of his friend, and his throat tightened.

"They've been following us the whole time," he said, feeling too stupid and defeated to breathe. "We just didn't realize it."

He jumped down the ladder and into the map car, with Ryle on his heels. He grabbed the PA and thumbed the mic. "Pez, make Lucille move faster!"

"But me and Vash just got engine one fixed."

"Then use engine two!"

"Please, boss," Pez pleaded over the speakers. "If I crank engine two up, Lucille might throw all her pistons, and she'd be a forty-ton paperweight."

"If you don't move now," Wyatt said, "we're going to be eaten by zombies!"

"What zombies? All I see is snow."

Now Pez was being blind on purpose, and Wyatt was

fed up with it. "Pez! Pull your head out of your butt and stick it out the window!"

A few seconds passed, followed by static, before Pez said, "Guess I'll be putting the pedal to the metal, boss."

"Music to my ears!" Wyatt hung up the mic. "Ready, Brakeman?"

But Ryle didn't seem to hear. Her eyes were focused on something he couldn't see. "They've been collecting zombies?" she said. "Maybe that's what Parcheesi meant when she talked about rounding up big herds."

"Don't play dumb," he said, feeling his chest tighten. "You were part of the whole plan, weren't you? The one that almost killed Cheddar."

"What?" Ryle drew back. "What are you talking about?"

"Think about it!" he said. "On our last loop through Denver, we saw maybe two or three dozen zombies in the whole city. This time, as soon as we got to the rail yards, they were lined up on the fences and overpasses. It *just happened* to be where we found the Dumpty in the Dolly Parton wig. You *happened* to be there. There *happened* to be deer carcasses against the fence!"

"That was all coincidence."

"That's what I told myself. But what if somebody else has been baiting zombies onto the loop? Parcheesi said the ferals had taken over the kids, but what if that isn't true?

What if she was a feral all along, and this was the scheme they had in mind?"

"That's insane," she said. "I didn't have any part in Diesel's mess. Please, Wy, I would never hurt Cheddar. I'm not a freaking feral. Don't think that of me."

Wyatt ran a hand through his hair. Of course he knew Ryle had nothing to do with Cheddar's getting hurt. "I'm sorry," he said, tears seeping from the corners of his eyes. There was just so much anger inside him, it felt like he been stabbed in the chest with a rusty nail.

She put a hand on his shoulder. "Hey, it's okay to be hurting over your friend. Just don't take it out on me, all right? We're on the same side."

"Yeah." He tugged his wristband. *Stand up.* Because that's what Ched would want him to do. "Same side."

"It's really not that bad, right?" she said. "Sure, every zombie on earth is coming at us, but the train is moving, and there's a billion feet of snow they've got to push through. Don't believe me, just look outside."

Wyatt glanced out the window, expecting to see a winter wonderland, but instead, there were multiple exhaust plumes rising into the air. Multiple trucks and SUVs were coming across the snowy fields. "No," he said. "It's really that bad."

"Huh?" Ryle looked out too. "Spoke too soon. Looks like Starla's boyfriend is coming for her, just like she threatened. They want Starla back. Probably our heads, too."

"They can't have either," Wyatt said. "Starla's going to Nirvana with us."

With a whistling sound, a projectile came over the horizon. It arced through the air and hit the ground a hundred yards down track.

Boom!

Chunks of dirt blew high into the air then rained down on the train.

Ryle put her fingers in her ringing ears. "What the heck was that?"

"Light Anti-tank Weapon," Wyatt said. "It's built to take out tanks. The good news is that it's a single-use launcher, and it's a pain to aim even up close. From that far away, it's even harder."

"What's the bad news?"

"I bet they have lots of LAWs." He headed for the sleeper cars. "Come on, Brakeman! I need your help!"

54

WYATT

Wyatt and Ryle burst into the last sleeper car, prepared to sound the alarm. Instead, they were met with menacing silence. Two kids were positioned at every window, their hunting bows armed and ready to fire from the frost-coated windows.

"Who gave the order to empty the armory?" Wyatt said.

Leroy turned, holding a speargun. "I thought you did."

Ryle threw her hands high. "Never point a weapon at anybody!" she said. "Even if it's not loaded."

"It's loaded." Leroy popped the bolt to prove it. "Big D gave us all harpoons."

"Diesel was here?" Wyatt caught Ryle's eye, and she flashed an *I told you so* look. "Hand it over, Leroy," he said forcefully. "Littles don't get weapons. Ever."

"Big D said you ordered it."

"I did not!" Wyatt yelled. This was insane! Someone shooting rockets at them was the real problem, but they still couldn't let Diesel get away with this.

"Kids!" Ryle commanded. "Give us everything back."

As the littles lined up to return the weapons, Wyatt noticed the quiet. The rocket fire had stopped. Maybe they were out of LAWs. Maybe not. Wyatt gathered the arrows in a cardboard box. He had collected a couple dozen before Diesel stormed into the carriage.

"What're you losers doing?" Diesel boomed, like he had every right to be there. "Leroy, I told you to get battle ready."

Ryle pointed her bō at him. Sweat streaked down her temples, and she swiped it away. "Nobody cares what you ordered," she said. "Traitor."

"Bring it on, hypocrite," Diesel said. "But first, let's tell everyone about Parcheesi's plan to steal the train. That's right. They told me your secret."

"Diesel, you might have killed my best friend and yours," Wyatt said, rage roiling within. How dare Diesel even show his face? "So speak up. Who's *they*, Diesel?"

"That's for me to know and you to find out." Diesel tossed a pair of handcuffs to Leroy. "Lock her up."

"I'm the conductor and you're under arrest, Diesel," Wyatt said, fighting the anger. "Leroy, give me the cuffs."

Leroy looked from Diesel to Wyatt to Diesel.

"Tell 'em, Ryle," Diesel said. "You've got the fever. Why fight zombies outside when one's already on the train."

"You sent Festus to spy on me," Ryle hissed. "I knew it."

"That moron?" Diesel said. "He couldn't even blow up the train right."

"Sounds like a confession to me," said Wyatt. "You're going to the caboose. Leroy, put the cuffs on him."

Diesel laughed. "Leroy's my boy. Why would he listen to you?"

"Because I'm the conductor," Wyatt said. "Because riders vow to follow the conductor's orders. Even you, Big D."

Diesel snatched the cuffs from Leroy. "Maybe it's time for a new conductor, bruh."

Suddenly it got as quiet inside as outside. Wyatt could hear the wheels on the tracks. The groaning of the cars as they swayed back and forth. Scary plumes of exhaust smoke rose from the plains. He had to stop Diesel before another rocket launched.

"Confiscate Ryle's fighting stick, Leroy," Diesel said.

Ryle handed it to him without a fight. "Careful. It's got a hair trigger."

Leroy looked at the bō, puzzled.

"There's no trigger, dummy," Diesel said, reaching for Ryle. "But now it's her turn for the caboose."

Before he could cuff her, Ryle snatched the bō back from Leroy and rammed the barrel against Diesel's cheek. "Take one step," she said, "and I'm putting another nostril in your face."

"There's scarier girls than you," Diesel said.

Wyatt raised his paintball gun, thinking it would make Diesel back off. He was a coward at heart. But when Wyatt met Diesel's eye, he saw something different—a hunger.

"Shoot me," Diesel said. "Do it!"

Wyatt fired a red paintball onto the ceiling. "Stand down!"

"I knew you didn't have the guts," Diesel said, laughing. "Like I told you, it's time for a new boss."

Wyatt shot him square in the forehead. "That's for Cheddar." He watched red paint ooze between Diesel's fingers as he screamed and covered the wound. "You don't have the guts to be conductor."

"If he doesn't," Starla said, "then what about me?" She rose from a seat in the back. Her hair was washed and trimmed. She wore clean clothes and held a speargun. "Drop the gun. And the stick."

Eyes on Starla, Ryle handed the staff to Leroy. Her eyes narrowed. "I knew you were a snake."

"I wouldn't call people names, since you're the ones who kidnapped me. But hey, turns out I like the train, so I'm taking it." Starla leveled the speargun at Ryle. "Say my name."

"Bite me," Ryle said.

Starla laughed. "Already did, *Ryle*."

"Put the speargun down," Wyatt said. "Before somebody gets hurt."

"That's the point, little brother. Now give Leroy the gun." Starla waited until Wyatt complied. "Here's how it's going to work. We stop the train, and you and the kiddies get off. Because I'm good people, we'll give you a head start before we turn the shamblers loose."

"We?" Wyatt said.

"Me, my boyfriend, and our feral friends. The ones shooting the rockets? Maybe now you'll learn some respect, *Ryle*."

"Wait," Ryle said, horrified. "You're doing this because I called you the wrong name?"

"Nah." Starla laughed. "I did it to get the train. All it took was telling Parcheesi to convince you and your friend to hijack it. Oh, and killing Marti so that wimpy Wyatt could take over."

And she pulled it off right under my nose, Wyatt thought. What a disaster. He couldn't believe that he hadn't seen it coming. He'd let everybody down. "Good plan," he said, trying to sound confident. "But I've got a better one. You and Diesel get off my train."

Starla laughed. "You kidnapped me to be a guinea pig. It was for the future of humanity, right? I might have said yes, if you'd asked."

"You never would've said yes," Ryle said.

"True, I never cared much for humanity." Starla snorted. The sound was sharp, with a mean edge to it. "Deez, stop playing with your boo-boo and go tell the engineer to stop the train."

"Deez?" Ryle laughed. "Sounds like a disease."

"Pez only follows my orders," Wyatt said.

"Take Wyatt with you, Deez."

"I can handle Pez myself," Diesel said, paint running down his nose.

"Don't make me tell you again." Starla pointed to the door. "Wyatt? I'm dead serious about harpooning Ryle if the train don't stop."

Wyatt knew she was serious. "What did she offer you, Deez?" Wyatt said as they headed toward the dining car.

"Her blood," Diesel said.

"You're a vampire now?"

"Not like that, moron. A blood transfusion. It'll make me immune like her. I get to live. You get to die."

"What? Have you got squat for brains? It won't work." Wyatt shook his head. "If you're the wrong blood type, you're dead as a doornail."

Diesel paused. "What's a doornail?"

RYLE

Five minutes later, with the train gaining speed, the door to the caboose vestibule swung open, and Leroy pointed a paintball gun at Ryle. "Inside."

"You're Starla's boy now." She peered into the cold darkness. Not much there but a footlocker and a door. "She's using you like she's using Diesel."

The paintball gun made a *bript* noise and left a streak of yellow paint as Leroy fired at the roof of the caboose. "Go inside, I said."

Leroy shoved her forward. He slammed the vestibule door. A chain clinked. He'd locked her in. She didn't even bother to test it.

"If you try to escape, I'll tell Starla," Leroy shouted.

"You do that, traitor." Ryle took a deep breath and knocked. Here goes nothing. "Hello? I need your help."

"Who are you?" A slot slid open. "What do you want?"

In the dim light, she could see only eyes. "I'm Ryle," she said, trying to stay calm. "You must be the nurse. I've been sent because I'm about to turn."

"Tell Wyatt you don't belong here," the nurse snarled. "You've got time left. Maybe weeks."

Weeks? Maybe long enough to make it to Nirvana. She

cursed herself for being so stupid. She'd convinced herself that she belonged in the caboose—probably because she didn't want to hurt anyone like her mom had. "Wyatt isn't the conductor anymore. The new conductor banished me."

The door swung open. The nurse was tall and hidden by shadows, and a hood covered his face. He smelled like boiled cafeteria cabbage.

"What were those explosions?" the nurse asked.

"Some ferals figured out how to launch rockets at us," Ryle said. "They're trying to blow up the train."

"Have they hit us yet?" The nurse's voice sounded hoarse, like he'd been coughing. "No, of course not. The train's still moving, right? We're picking up speed."

"Where are the others?" Ryle asked. As her eyes adjusted to the dim light, she could see that the cages were all empty. "Wyatt said the Council was back here."

"They were gone too far," the nurse said. "I had to put them off last night. "

"Does 'put them off' mean what I think it does?"

The nurse nodded.

"Does Wyatt know?"

"Wyatt sticks to his business, and I stick to mine. It works better that way."

"That's the thing. He can't tend to business because the train's been hijacked by this girl and her feral friends."

"The immune girl?"

"Yeah, and I was hoping you'd have some good ideas for getting Lucille back. Since we're surrounded by zombies, and Starla is about to kick everyone off."

"I can only think of one good idea when you're losing a fight."

"What would that be?" Ryle asked.

"Fight harder." The nurse opened the hatch, and light filled the caboose, so bright it was hard to see anything but the sky above. He handed her a gaff. "They think you're out of the game. Use that against them."

"Wait," she said, shielding her eyes, "there's something I need to tell you. It's about the cure."

She could see the nurse's face now. All of it. It was no longer hidden in shadows, the hood pulled back. She recoiled and instinctively reached for the bō. But then she recognized something, even if his skin was rotting. His bright eyes looked familiar and so did the quick but sad smile. Being a zombie couldn't change that.

"There isn't a cure," the nurse said. "We went over this a thousand times with Cheddar. You can't go back once you've started to turn."

"Yeah, but what about you?"

"Cheddar says I'm the 'anomaly.' Which means it's just taking me longer to turn, and you don't want that."

"Looks like you're not such an anomaly at all. We've heard other zombies talk. There was even one whose

dentures Wyatt stole, and it kept demanding them back."
She laughed. "Teef! Teef! Sorry. You had to be there."

"What's your point?"

"My point is," she said, "hang on a little bit longer. I
know—"

"You don't know me! If I let the monster out, I can't put
it back in."

"But you can talk. You can think. You can control
yourself."

"A dog with rabies can control itself, too. Until it can't."

Ryle squeezed her eyes shut. "Why won't you listen?
There's an answer, and it's *this close*."

"We were always *this close*!" The nurse pounded his chest.
"I was *this close*, but the parasite got me anyway." Then he
flashed that sad smile. "It'll get you, too."

"Then it gets me. But I'm through with doing the wrong
thing for the right reason, and until I turn, I'm going to
hang on. You should, too."

The nurse laughed ruefully. "You think Starla is lucky,
but she gets to watch everybody else die. It's over for me.
Ask Cheddar."

"I can't do that." Ryle shook her head. "Cheddar almost
died in the explosion. He's still unconscious."

"W-what?" The nurse took a step back. He buried his
face in his hands, then shook his head ferociously. "Not
Ched Man. How did that happen?"

Ryle wanted to say how sorry she was but knew the nurse didn't care what she thought. "Festus sabotaged the engine on Diesel's orders, but Starla was behind the whole thing. The sabotage. The hijacking. The rocket attacks. Cheddar's almost dying. All of it. Please," she begged, "help me take Lucille back."

The nurse pulled the hood down over his face, hiding it again, and Ryle wished that she could help him. So much pain. But there was nothing she could do now but follow the nurse's advice and rejoin the fight.

She sighed and pushed the gaff up through the open hatch. "I'm going, but I'm not giving up on you, Pike. You're Wyatt's brother, and you're all the family he's got left."

56

WYATT

"Don't try nothing funny, bruh," Diesel warned Wyatt on the way to the locomotive.

Wyatt had not been up to anything except formulating a plan. To get the speargun from Diesel. To take Diesel back to Starla to disarm her. But he had to wait till Diesel's guard was down. He put his hands in the air. He kept his eyes locked ahead and walked as slowly as possible. In school, they called it slow-walking, and teachers hated it.

They reached the fuel tank car, but instead of the usual jump over to the locomotive, Wyatt went down the ladder deliberately. Diesel practically had smoke coming out of his ears when they reached the snow-covered deck.

"You're going to pay for hurting Cheddar and Festus," Wyatt said. "*Bruh.*"

"You shot my face and got my ear bit off. I owed you." Diesel scoffed. "Like you even care about Festus. And your boy Ched was in the wrong place at the wrong time. That's not on me."

Wyatt ground his teeth like he had a mouthful of glass. "It's stuck on you like your awful BO."

"Shut up," Diesel said. "You're just trying to stall by making me mad. Hurry it up."

"I agree," said Starla. "It took you guys forever." She sat on the locomotive rail, trying to keep her balance. "Like a couple of turtles."

"How'd you get here?" Diesel said, clearly surprised to see her.

"She ran the roofs, obviously," Wyatt said. "Where's Ryle, Starla? I promise you, if you hurt her—"

"Oh, honey, if I wanted to hurt her, I already would've." Starla brushed the hair from her face. "But since you're curious, Leroy escorted Ryle to the caboose."

"The caboose?" Wyatt snapped.

"That's where you send kids who are turning, right?" She smirked and tapped her nose. "Don't deny it. I know a zombie when I smell one."

At least Starla hadn't shot Ryle, and the nurse wouldn't hurt her. He'd be able to free her later. He glared at Starla. "You sent us for Pez. Why are you here?"

"Honestly?" she said. "I was coming up to meet the engineer, but I'll be punishing Deez instead."

"What?" Diesel said, his voice squeaking. "Why would you punish me? I did everything you told me to."

"Yeah, no," she said. "I didn't tell you to get Cheddar hurt, did I? That kid's the brains of this operation. We needed him. He's half the reason I even wanted this rolling rust bucket."

"But, but . . ." Diesel sputtered. "You've got me. I had

Festus blow up the engine. I signaled for the archers to shoot Ryle. I—"

"Screwed up," she said. "Give me your speargun."

Diesel handed it over. "But I need it."

"I'm sure you do." She backed him up to the edge of the deck, then fired a harpoon into his thigh. "That's for Parcheesi."

Diesel screamed as he fell backward. He landed awkwardly on the railbed, then tumbled into a snowdrift, too dazed to stand. Lucille rolled on, leaving him behind, and Wyatt had to look away as memories of Ricky chasing the train filled his mind.

"You going to miss old Deez?"

"Not really," Wyatt said.

"Me neither."

"What now?" Wyatt said.

"Yeah, I was asking myself the same question." She cocked her head and nodded. "I guess it's time for you and yours to get off my train."

"What about Cheddar and Festus? They're too hurt to move."

"I said everybody. Except for the engineer, of course. He'll be staying."

"Pez won't do that," Wyatt said.

"I'll make it worth his while. Get him out here."

"Pez," Wyatt called into the engineer's cab. "Come on out."

A few seconds later Pez stormed outside. "What's going on?" His eyes almost bugged out. "Why ain't you answering the PA? There's two trucks with rockets up ahead!"

Two trucks? Probably more of Starla's friends. Wyatt held up his hands. "Sorry, I was kind of busy. Starla wants us all off the train, so go make the announcement to abandon ship."

Pez looked at Starla, then back at Wyatt. He bit his lip, shook his head ruefully, then returned to the cab. Starla gestured with the speargun for Wyatt to follow, and she brought up the rear. Pez cursed her under his breath.

"Make the call," Wyatt said. "It's going to be okay."

Pez grabbed the mic and thumbed it. "All riders—abandon ship!" Then he threw the mic across the cab, barely missing Starla's head.

57

WYATT

With the zombies surrounding the whole train, Lucille kept gaining speed, and the herd began slipping behind. But the ferals' trucks—a red Tundra and a massive gold Hummer—were now running parallel to the tracks, the zombie herd parting to make a path. Wyatt knew time was running out. They couldn't abandon Cheddar and Festus, and if they were moved, it might kill them.

"Trust me," Wyatt whispered to Pez. "Don't give up. Ched is counting on us."

"I can't do this," Pez said and started crying. "Lucille is all I got left."

"It's okay, baby." Starla patted his hand. "I know how much you love this toy. As a matter of fact, I'm keeping you while all your friends jump. We need somebody to run the engine."

"Locomotive," Pez said through tears. "And ain't."

Starla smiled. "You'd be surprised how I motivate people."

"Motivate this!" Vash howled, bursting from a storage closet and tackling Starla. The punch caught Starla right under the ear, and she dropped the speargun, staggering backward.

Wyatt kicked the speargun away. "It's over," he said, pushing Vash behind him to keep her from throwing another punch. Before Starla could get her bearings, Wyatt marched her down the corridor and outside to the deck. "Signal your ferals to back off."

Starla pressed a hand against her sore jaw. "Didn't think you had it in you, Wyatt."

"I had it in me!" Vash yelled, coming through the engine room door. "Come get some more!"

She started for Starla, but Pez came up behind and bear-hugged her.

"Signal them to stand down," Wyatt repeated.

Starla huffed and raised her arms in an X. "There you go."

But the trucks didn't back off. They veered sharply to the north, then turned around, aiming straight for Lucille. With a puff of smoke, a rocket launched, and Starla started laughing.

Wyatt hit the deck as the rocket whistled over the train. It landed close, thirty feet away, and sprayed the entire locomotive with debris. Vash shook rocks off her shirt, and Pez pulled chunks of snow and prairie grass from his hair.

Starla, who hadn't ducked, caught the brunt of it. "You stupid moron idiot dorks!" she yelled, wiping her face, her fingers coming away with blood and dirt. Her right eye puffed up, and muddy tears were streaming from it. "You weren't supposed to hit me!"

The gold Hummer crested an embankment ahead. A voice came over a loudspeaker mounted on top. "Throw down your weapons! Or we'll fire more rockets!"

The Hummer speakers squawked again, but the command was drowned out by the Tundra gunning to join it. They all came to a halt ahead of the train, which was still gaining speed as the first Big Ten Curve came into view.

The ferals jumped down from their trucks. Wyatt counted thirteen kids, all of them in some kind of battle gear. There were a couple of tall ones, but most were young. Even if they did look small, their weapons did not.

Out of the corner of his eye, Wyatt saw Vash elbow Pez hard and mouth, "Now?"

Pez shook his head. "Thanks to Wyatt," he whispered, "we've got them right where we want them."

58

WYATT

A tall zombie leapt from the Hummer—a massive, gas-guzzling relic decked out with gold paint, spinning rims, and a light rack full of animal carcasses. It looked like something from a bad goth metal concert, and so did the driver. He was tall and slender, with long hair draped over his shoulders. He dressed in a black duster and wore a red bandana.

"Lich!" Starla glared at Wyatt, then smiled. "Now you brats are in trouble."

"That's one tall zombie," Vash said.

Who looks very familiar, Wyatt thought.

Lich loped alongside the train, then bounded up to the locomotive deck, moving with easy grace. Now that he was close, Wyatt could see his eyes. The pupils were dilated and oozing gunk, and his skin was sallow and pitted.

I know him, Wyatt thought. One of the Council. The first one to try the blood serum. The first one to be abandoned. "Ricky? Is that you?"

"Don't call him that!" Starla elbowed Wyatt in the gut. "His name is Lich!"

Wyatt barely blinked before Lich was on them. He moved impossibly fast. His incredibly long arms reaching for Starla. His spidery hand removing the speargun from her grip. His gnarled finger pulled the trigger as he aimed at Wyatt.

Click.

Click, click.

"Nur?" Lich said and looked down the barrel. "Jummed?"

"I can fix that for you," Wyatt said.

Lich swatted Wyatt with the stock, and Wyatt felt a quick sting and angry ants of pain crawled down his shoulder. Lich swung again, but Wyatt ducked and punched him in the ribs. There was the crack of bones breaking.

"Ow!" Wyatt said and pulled his fist back, a bloody gash across his fingers.

Lich's eyes went wide, and he licked his lips like he'd seen a tasty treat. "Nom, nom."

"Cover the blood, idiot!" Starla ordered, stepping between Lich and Wyatt, her arms out wide. She wrapped them around Lich. "No noms yet," she said. "I promise you lots of treats later."

But Lich looked famished. He yanked the red handkerchief off, revealing a rotted face. His nose was gone, his cheeks just tendons that connected bone. His tongue danced between his teeth, licking the air.

"Holy moly," Vash said. "Ain't never seen nothing so disgusting in all my freaking life."

"Shut your mouth!" Starla said. "He's beautiful."

Wyatt grabbed Starla's speargun and tossed it aside, wincing at the pain in his shoulder. "Get off this train right now!"

"He won't shoot us, Lich," Starla said. "He doesn't have the guts. None of them do."

"Hey! I'd be glad to shoot you both twice," Vash said. "Three times, if you want. Right, Wyatt?"

"Why-yut? Why-yut!" Lich tore his eyes away from Wyatt's wound. "Hates shu! Hates shu!" Lich turned toward the zombie swarm and made an X with his arms. "Shood Why-ut! Far duh luckit!"

Far duh luckit? Wyatt thought. *Fire the rocket!* "Take cover!" he yelled.

Wyatt, Vash, and Pez dived inside the engine room as three booms sounded. All around them, the cab windows shook, and the metal floor bucked. Wyatt squeezed his eyes closed and pulled his friends close to protect them.

Seconds after the shelling began, it was over. When Vash and Pez tried to get up, Wyatt held them down. "Stay still," he whispered.

"Lich, why did you do that?" Starla's weary voice came from the deck outside. "Are you trying to kill me?"

Wyatt peeked through a shattered window and saw Starla shake debris from her hair while blood bloomed across her shoulder.

She looked at the blood and touched it with her fingers.

"Lich, don't even think of eating me."

"I hope he does," Vash whispered. "Would serve her right."

"True," Wyatt said, "but she's tougher than she looks."

"She ain't tough," Pez said. "She's just mean."

"No matter what she is," Wyatt said, "we have to get rid of her. Pez, is the plan a go?"

Pez nodded. "But we've got to uncouple the cars fast, or Lucille's got no chance of making the Big Ten Curve."

"Leave that to me," Wyatt said and got up. "I helped my brother and Ched design the plan."

Pez grabbed Wyatt's shirttail. "Hold on. How're you gonna get past Starla?"

Before he could answer, Starla barked, "Do what I say or I'll skin you all alive!" then suddenly, there was silence.

59

WYATT

Wyatt peered out the engine cab window, his breath fogging the shattered remnants of the glass. Like lumbering, stilted locusts, the herd advanced through the snow, drawn to the train as if Lich was the queen bee of an entire hive.

"Something's going on," Vash whispered as she and Pez ducked beside him. "Why's it so quiet all of a sudden?"

Wyatt hunkered back down. "There's a herd of shamblers about to reach us, all headed toward Starla's boyfriend."

"Maybe they want to eat him?" Vash said.

"I think he's giving them orders. I think he and Starla are going out to meet them."

"Makes no sense," Pez said. "Zombies have no brains left for orders."

"They can't talk, either," Vash said. "But Lich does."

Wyatt looked again, just as the herd reached the tracks, then turned as one for the train. Zombies hit the sides of the cars, and their gnarled fingers scratched the metal skin of the exterior as they tried to grab hold. But they slid off the freezing metal and tumbled under the wheels.

"We can't stop them," Wyatt said, but he felt paralyzed watching the carnage.

"What's going on?" Vash popped up, too. "Holy-zombie-moly!"

Then with that horrible keening scream, a zombie fresh covered in a blanket of snow flung itself against the windows of the sightseer car, and there was an awful crack. The windows shattered. Glass shards blew out like deadly snowflakes, and Wyatt heard the littles shriek. Then suddenly the zombie fresh flew back out the window, followed by a barrage of luggage, cutlery, shoes, and even a half-eaten sandwich.

"Woo-hoo!" Vash yelled. "They're fighting back! That's my family right there!"

But Wyatt knew the littles were just buying time. They could only hold off the zombies for so long until a few fresh got through, and then—he didn't want to think about it.

The horn sounded, and Pez pointed ahead. "Shamblers at twelve o'clock!!"

As if pushed by the winds, zombies flooded the train tracks. They stopped and looked up, like they were confused. For a moment, everything felt weirdly quiet and still.

Then Lucille slammed into them, plowing through wave after wave of zombies. Wyatt felt the entire locomotive shudder as it blew through the herd. He looked at the control panel, which was lighting up with failure warnings like the Fourth of July. With every passing second, more zombies smashed on the train's hull.

"Lucille can't take this!" Pez hollered. "She's gonna derail!"

"We've got to shake the rotters in back, too!" Vash yelled.

Pez's hand hovered over the emergency brake button. "We gotta stop!"

"No!" Wyatt pulled Pez's hand away. "We've got to go faster, or we won't make the Big Ten!"

"Won't matter if we derail, boss!"

"Then it's time!" Wyatt yelled. "Are the turbos set for override?"

"All I got to do is press a button."

"Then lock yourself in the engineer's cab," Wyatt said. "We'll handle the rest!"

"I druther let Lucille blow up," Pez said, "than leave my friends behind!"

"And we feel the same way." Vash punched his shoulder. "Lock the door and don't budge until you get Wyatt's signal."

"Don't take all day!" Pez said.

"You know," Vash said as she shut the door on him, "that boy ain't so bad once you get past all the grease. What now, Conductor?"

"First we distract the zombies." Wyatt rummaged through Pez's toolbox until he found a bottle of fuel cleaner and a torch lighter. He stuffed a rag inside the bottle. "Then we find Ryle."

"Thought you forgot about her."

"Never! She's my brakeman!" He ran out onto the deck, lit the rag, and fired the bottle into the zombie swarm.

The bottle arced through the air, landing in the middle of the herd. It shattered, and bright flames exploded with a whoosh, spreading quickly. The zombies stumbled back, their movements herky-jerky as they stampeded away from the train. For an instant, the fire seemed to be alive, dancing and flickering over the snow.

"Smells like a zombie fry!" Vash yelled as she and Wyatt ran the roofs to the dining car, where they heard loud screams. "There's a fight!" she said, pointing at a feral falling from a window below them.

With a crash, a second feral flew through a window.

"Somebody's mad!" Vash said.

"Hope they're on our side!" Wyatt said as they slid down the ladder and entered the dining car.

There were little ones lined up on either side of the car. In the middle of the chaos stood Ryle, holding a cast-iron skillet. She was covered in sweat, and blood trickled from her nose.

"You, Ryle!" Vash yelled. "What's going on, girl? Did you toss those ferals out the window?"

Ryle's eyes flicked toward Vash and Wyatt, who grabbed

a PA mic and yelled, "Pez! Hit it!"

A few seconds later, there was a small boom, followed by a calamitous *hw-w-hww-wh-whomp!*

And Lucille took off like a rocket.

The world outside became a blur, and the brute force of the acceleration knocked everyone down, made everyone scream bloody murder.

"Are you trying to kill us?" Ryle yelled at Wyatt.

"It's okay!" he yelled back. "It's a great plan!"

The plan was a maneuver Cheddar had designed. If the train ever needed to make a quick escape, they'd pump unspent fuel into the lines, overloading Lucille's turbochargers—like a dose of nitrous to a race car. The boiler might blow up or Lucille might bounce off the rails, but there was also a chance, Cheddar had calculated, that the fuel would hit the turbos with enough force that they would practically fly.

Lucille was flying!

"Let's go!" Wyatt pulled Ryle to her feet. "Vash, move them to the sleeping car, got it?"

Vash nodded and started shepherding the littles out. "You heard the conductor, people, let's move!"

"Tell me what's going on?" Ryle asked, waving the skillet at him.

Quickly, Wyatt explained the plan.

"And half the train has to go?" Ryle said.

"More than half," Wyatt said. "Every car behind the infirmary has to go." The infirmary. He thought about Cheddar lying unconscious. This was his plan, and Wyatt was going to make it work. "Otherwise, the train's too long to pull through the Big Ten Curve. Inertia would throw us clean off the tracks!"

Lucille's momentum was slowing. Wyatt could feel it. He could feel the clock speeding up, too, every second slipping away, bringing them closer to disaster. "Let's move!"

He sprinted toward the back of the train, Ryle close behind him, shouting, "Hurry! Hurry! Hurry!" until he slammed through the vestibule between the infirmary and the first sleeper carriage.

He pointed to the coupling. "We need to uncouple these cars!"

"What about the caboose?" Ryle demanded. "We fought so hard to keep it."

Wyatt took a breath to calm himself. "It has to go."

"What about me?" she asked. "Do I have to go, too?"

Tears were welling in her eyes. They were bloodshot and tinged with red, and the irises were dilated. Now it made sense. Her sudden strength. The way she'd beaten those ferals, throwing them outside like rag dolls.

"You're close," Wyatt yelled, "but you haven't turned yet." He tried to make it sound straightforward, but the fear seeped from his voice. "Maybe you'll be lucky like Starla."

"Dream on!" Ryle said. "Hey! Take care of Vash and my littles. They're the only family I've got left. Well, and maybe Cheddar and Pez. You, I'm not so sure about." She laughed. "Promise me you'll get them all to—"

She couldn't say the word.

"We do this together, or we don't do it at all." Wyatt shook his head. "That's an order, Brakeman."

"You are such a—" She bit the word off and angrily shook her head. "Fine, let's do this. What's first?"

"We have to manually close the angle cock on the coupling," he yelled and pointed to the mechanism. "I've done it lots of times."

He hooked his elbow through the railing and reached down to pull the cut-lever up. Then lifted the lock to release the couplers. He tried to pull the pin, but it was frozen tight.

"Move!" Ryle yelled and jumped to the other side of the coupling.

She hammered the ice with the skillet. The pin popped up, and Wyatt yanked it free. The air hose separated, the two ends whipping like an angry rattler, and the coupling broke apart all too easily.

The unhooked cars quickly lost speed. One second Wyatt was looking at Ryle's face, and the next a chasm was opening between the two halves of the train.

"Jump!" Wyatt yelled and waved for her to join him. "You can make it!"

"There's no happy ending for me," she yelled back. "Sooner or later, we all end up in the caboose."

"Not everybody!" Pike called as he swung down beside Ryle. Before she could react, he took her by the shoulders, and they flew through the air. Then Pike was swinging her onto the ladder and climbing past her to the roof of the infirmary.

"Jerk face!" she screamed, shaking the skillet at Pike. "You messed up my exit!"

"I hate sappy endings!" he called back.

Suddenly there was the scream of an engine, and the tricked-out Hummer roared up alongside the abandoned cars. Wyatt could see Lich driving the Hummer, but he didn't see Starla.

Lich swerved hard to the left, and a feral kid wormed his way out a back window. He was holding a LAW. The Hummer slowed down, and the feral gunner took aim.

An instant later the caboose exploded, shattering every window, blowing holes through the roof, and blowing the doors a hundred feet into the sky.

"Lich really hates that caboose," Ryle said.

Wyatt shrugged. "He was its first prisoner."

The Hummer's engine revved, and it caught up with the train again. The feral gunner leaned out the back window and aimed the LAW at Wyatt and Ryle.

"Get down!" Wyatt yelled.

They ducked as the shell blew past them, barely missing the last car, then exploded harmlessly in an open field as Lucille entered the first Big Ten Curve and roared around it, steel wheels singing. For a second the whole train lifted off the rails.

Then with a loud *wham*, the wheels settled, and Lucille kept going.

"Yes!" Ryle shouted and pumped her fist.

"That almost gave me a heart attack," Wyatt whispered.

Right behind them, the Hummer skidded around the curve, following the tracks, blowing snow and debris behind it. Then it cut across onto a long stretch of access road that ran beside the tracks. For a moment the Hummer drew so close to the train, Wyatt could see Lich.

"We can't shake them!" Ryle yelled.

"We'll be safe after we make it past the Coal Creek Canyon bridge," Wyatt yelled back. "The road ends, and the tracks go into the mountains. They won't be able to follow us."

The Hummer accelerated and swerved closer. The gunner leaned out the window.

There's no way he'll miss this time, Wyatt realized. It was point-blank range.

"Leave my family alone!" Pike bellowed. He dived from

the top of the infirmary car, his duster catching the wind like a cape, and landed on the roof of the Hummer.

The Hummer swerved, clearly trying to shake Pike. He hung on tight as the vehicle fought the snowdrifts, bouncing through the frozen bed of Coal Creek.

"Look!" Ryle yelled, pointing to Pike kneeling on the Hummer's roof. "What's he doing?"

Pike raised a hand in salute as the Hummer bounced from the creek bed and onto Coal Creek Canyon Road. Then he swung down through the rear window. Then the back door flew open, and the feral gunner came flying out as the train crossed the bridge over Coal Creek Road.

A few seconds later, Wyatt saw Pike in the front seat, fighting Lich for the steering wheel.

Lich tried break away, but Pike sank his teeth into Lich's neck and tore off a chunk of flesh. He opened his gaping, bloody mouth to take another bite, and Wyatt realized that there was no longer any hope for his brother.

The Hummer veered back onto Coal Creek Road, tires chewing up the snow, the rear end fishtailing. It careened around a sharp curve, headed straight for a narrow railroad bridge made of crumbling steel and concrete. Too narrow for the Hummer's six-foot-wide frame.

A hundred yards away.

Seventy.

Fifty.

Twenty.

"They're not slowing down!" Ryle gasped. "They can't clear that opening!"

"No!" Wyatt shouted. "Pike! Hit the brakes!"

The Hummer skidded, tires screaming. The vehicle flipped onto two wheels, then rolled, and slammed into the bridge's concrete pillars at full speed.

The explosion set a geyser of flames into the sky. Another explosion, this one louder, lifted the Hummer off the ground and tore it apart like a toy. Tar-like smoke billowed from the wreckage.

In a heartbeat, they were gone.

Wyatt bowed his head. Minute after minute passed by. He closed his eyes, not hearing or feeling.

"Oh, no. Wyatt, your brother . . . the Hummer just . . . " Ryle coughed and staggered over to Wyatt. "I'm so sorry."

Wordlessly, Wyatt reached for her hand and pulled her beside him. Tears poured down his face, and she wrapped her arms around him. It wasn't much solace for a boy who had lost a brother, but it was all she could do for him, and she said a silent prayer that it would be enough.

Ryle was about to stand when a burned and bleeding hand grabbed the top rail of the ladder. She looked up to see an impossible face.

"No way," she said. "We just watched you blow up."

Lich heaved himself onto the roof. His clothes were

smoldering, and half his face had been burnt off. Oily black blood oozed out, but he didn't seem to notice. "Lich zump dout," he growled.

Ryle stood and waved the cast-iron skillet up like a tennis racket. "Take your best shot, pus face."

"Lichs gonna ead yer braaains!" Lich screeched and lurched forward.

"There'll be no brains eating, Ricky," Ryle said and flung the skillet. "Catch!"

Clang!

The skillet bounced off Lich's head, and he toppled backward, pinwheeling his arms and howling. He grasped for the ladder, but there was nothing under him but air. He landed in a deep snowbank and disappeared.

"So long, zombie king!" Ryle said, waving so long. "Things just didn't pan out for you."

"Nice swing, Brakeman," Wyatt said quietly.

Ryle spun around. "I completely forgot you were there!"

Wyatt shook his head. "Didn't pan out for him?"

"Oh, no, I mean, I am so sorry for being a jerk." She covered her mouth. "You just lost your brother, and your best friend's hurt, and I'm making skillet puns."

"It was hilarious," he said. "Pike would've loved it. He always did hate sappy endings."

60

CABOOSE

When things had settled down enough, when what remained of the zombie train had heaved her way through the Big Ten turns and topped the Continental Divide, Wyatt and Ryle grabbed a few cookies and made their way to the helipad, the two of them in the moonlight, sitting atop a train full of kids surviving the zombie apocalypse, bound for Utah.

"Y'know, the tracks over that bridge were probably destroyed in the explosion," she said, scraping the creamy center from her Oreo. "The train won't be able to run the loop anymore."

"It doesn't need to," he said. "There's no going back to how it used to be."

"I'm glad Festus is doing better. I kind of missed that little rat."

"Me, too," Wyatt said. Festus had come to during the fight. Cheddar still was not awake, but Ginny was hopeful. So was Wyatt.

Ryle popped the cookie into her mouth. "I'm so hungry! Turning into a zombie makes you famished."

"Please don't eat my face," Wyatt said.

"Nah, you'd taste like chicken," Ryle said and laughed.

"What are we going to do without Starla? There's no point going into Nirvana now."

"That's not true," Wyatt said. "I mean, those scientists don't know Starla exists. They've probably found immune kids by now. She wasn't that special."

"Oh, she was special," Ryle said and held out her fist. When Wyatt bumped it, she made an explosion noise and waggled her fingers.

"Thought that was a you-and-Vash thing," he said.

"Now it's a zombie train thing."

They sat side by side and stared at the sky. Stars filled every corner with brilliant light, and a great horned owl soared in growing circles above the canyons. There was no guarantee that Ryle or any of them would reach Seattle, but Wyatt was willing to take that bet. Even if he was wrong, another conductor would lead the train, and in time, they would find a cure. The zombie train would never stop.

"Sorry to buzz kill your special moment," Vash said, coming up the ladder. "But me and Tater got something to show you."

Ryle groaned. "Can it wait?"

"It's better than a Christmas present."

"Fiiine."

Wyatt looked at Vash and Tater. Sandwiched between them was Starla, bedraggled and not so defiant. His heart sank, then it did a flip. The miracle girl was still alive.

"We found her in Diesel's room," Vash said. "Hunkered down, eating all the Snickers bars Big D stole."

"I was hungry," Starla whined. "What do you dorks expect a girl to do when she's starving?"

"To clean up after herself," Tater growled, and folded his arms.

"Well, I'm all for purging her now," Vash said. "I'll even give her a push in the right direction."

Everybody laughed except Starla.

"That's not funny," she said.

"It's a little funny," Ryle said.

"It's a lot funny," Vash said.

"Y'all know we can't purge her," Wyatt said.

"She wanted to blow Lucille up," Vash said. "I can't forgive that." She wrinkled up her nose. "I also don't like her face."

Wyatt turned to Ryle. "What do you think?"

Ryle sighed and shook her head. "Starla, I like you even less than Vash does, but you're our best chance for a cure, so I think we should let you stay."

Starla's jaw dropped. "Did not see that coming."

"Under whatever conditions the Council sets," Wyatt said. "That's the deal. Agree to it or leave. Now. Make your choice."

Starla touched her injured shoulder. She was still hurting, hungry, alone. But if there was one thing Wyatt knew about Starla—she was a survivor. "Whatever," she finally said. "I guess I can handle you dorks till we get to that lab or whatever."

"Fair enough," Wyatt said. "Go with Tater. He'll get you real food and find a place for you to sleep."

"Like the caboose," Tater grumbled, steering Starla to the ladder.

"You ain't got no caboose," she said as she climbed down.

"We can find another one," Tater said. "Just for you."

Vash watched them go. "There's more news." She bit her bottom lip, like she was trying to hold something in. "It's about Cheddar."

Oh, no, Wyatt thought and braced himself for the worst. "How bad is it?"

"Well," Vash said, after what felt like forever. "Cheddar's awake." Then the smile she'd been squelching bloomed across her face. "And he's been asking to see his one and only best friend. He says he's got plans for Nirvana."